DANI

C. F. FRANK

OTHER TITLES BY C. F. FRANK

SONGS FOR REYNA (2019)

COUNTY OF KINGS (2019)

LONG LIVE, KING (2020)

ENTIME (WINTER 2021)

THE FACE (WINTER 2022)

THE HIDDEN (COMING SOON)

Printed in the United States of America

First Printing, 2018

ISBN-10: 172649635X
ISBN-13: 978-1726496353

For Mother

CHAPTER I

What a day it is to be alive! What a day to be anything!

SOMEWHERE RIGHT AT THIS VERY MOMENT someone has an idea. On a day similar to one such as this, someone will act on their ideas. Some of those ideas will be to change the world. Some will even change the balance of power or even their account balances. Nonetheless, someone somewhere has ideas. But look at you! Without any collusion or interference at all someone right now is making a change. They are fulfilling purpose and discovering doors that were once unseen. They are capturing greatness!

Yes, someone somewhere amongst the sovereign is making life altering decisions with their ideas that may inextricably affect the apolitical. Maybe it has nothing to do with the world, or even caring anything about making a difference. Maybe it's just in the favor of their own self interests.

Maybe it's the material things, the allure, the status, or the power that comes with newfound success stories. Maybe it's just capturing one's goals. However, they're all capitalizing on everything they have prepared and trained hours for. At this very moment it's happening, but look at you! While you sit here on your lazy ass whining, griping, moaning, and debating what you are willing or not willing to sacrifice for this moment. Pathetic!

I can see the smiles on all of their faces—the even-keeled. I can see sun rays illuminating the entire room of a majestic office. Within its twenty-three by fourteen-foot space discourse meets action and congeniality. It's a space trying desperately to contain the ambitious and the audacious alike.

Yes, I can hear and feel the pleasantries ingratiating a new dawn of many fruitful and lucrative relationships. The relationships that allow entry to spaces unencumbered by anything less than the savant and wunderkinds. I can see it, and I want all of it. At this very moment I am willing to sacrifice everything for it! Whatever I have to sacrifice, I will. I'll do it for that very feeling. Franklin Mitchell did this every morning. It was his ritual.

It was seven thirty in the morning as Franklin Mitchell, a thirty-something-year-old married executive and father, allowed his mind to do as it always did early in the morning. He was having an out of body experience. It was said to be borderline ranting if you asked his seventeen-year-old daughter. But as Franklin continued to sip his morning coffee, it was his early morning 'pep talk' to himself. Those thoughts were his "motivational vitals" as he called them. Franklin was a man focused more on his own personal goals than he had ever been at any point in his life.

Just as an Olympic sprinter is focused on the vertical plane of a finish line, Franklin too was fixated with his own version of gold medal glory.

Through his transient state he was able to hear his father words, 'Money holds no weight to a man who keeps his word and stands for what's right. That is even when it isn't the easiest thing to do. What good is all the money or success in the world to the sanctimonious or misanthropic?'

Arthur A. Mitchell, Franklin's father, was a proud and perplexing man. He also was one of two original founders of Mitchell, Leonard, and Maxwell, a non-depository institution specializing in securities brokerage and investment advisory services.

Franklin could visualize his father's senescent face and bleary disposition. He's the only man he had ever idolized and emulated. Though he often despised Arthur throughout his youth.

' *What does he think of my ambition now? What would he think to know I'm the same as him through and through? What would he say if he knew the same obsession that burns within him burns deep within me as well? It's the absolute same obsession that caused our strained and oscillated relationship. It's the same obsession that alienated my mother and nearly destroyed our family. The same obsession that sacrificed occasional weekends and holidays with the family that runs in me as well. Is it possible the more I try not to be my father that I am on a fast track of becoming him?'* Franklin thought to himself.

Suddenly, a vibrant young woman in her late teens rushed down the long staircase into the kitchen. Her abrupt presence was more than enough to redirect Franklin's focus from his intrapersonal concerns to accept her caring embrace. The five-eight-star athlete was Franklin's daughter. Being that she was a senior of St. Lucas High School, a private Roman Catholic high school in the center of the city, she was always up and at it around this time. The caramel complected fun-loving belle was the most sensible out of the family of three oftentimes.

Her full name was Danielle Cora Mitchell. More often than not she was referred to as "Dani" by all of her teammates, friends, and family. It was her grandmother, Mrs. Denise Ana Mitchell, who coined her nickname when she was a toddler. Heavily involved in extracurricular activities, Dani always had a competitive spirit and enthralling way about her.

Being a high school letterman in volleyball and track and field were a few reasons why she was often up so early. All of her teachers, instructors, and coaches considered her to be the prototypical student if ever there was one. It was safe to say that Dani was highly regarded as being one of the school's most well-liked pupils.

"Good morning, Daddy!" she said happily.

"Uh, oh, there she is! Five-seven, hailing from the great state of Georgia weighing in at—"

"Cut it out, Dad," she said laughingly. "And I'm actually five-eight!"

Franklin's cheeks turned flamingo pink.

"Good morning, darling. How are you?" Franklin

asked in a rather exuberant way. "Did you get a good night's rest?"

"Yes, I was able to hibernate very well, Dad," she said sarcastically with a smile. "I now know that you will always keep the temperature in our humble home well below zero in the evening."

"Well, if you ever have trouble finding me, I'll always be in the coldest area baby girl," he said. "You know I can't stand the heat. Our people are from the tropics, but it doesn't mean I have to like it."

Dani chuckled in amusement.

"Dad, I have to run," she cut in. "Before I do, you do remember that my final home game is in two days, right? The playoffs begin soon too. Out of all the games you have or could miss, I would love for you not to miss this one, okay?!

"If you're working late or whatever then it's fine, I guess. But I really want you and mom both there. So, you'll be there, right?"

"Yes, I will be there, and I'll be the loudest fan in the stands," Franklin boasted.

"Great! By the way, stop ranting will you!" she shouted before exiting.

Dani grabbed a bottled water and energy bar from the refrigerator and hugged Franklin goodbye.

A small smirk formed on his face as he watched her leave the room.

She screamed her goodbyes before walking out the front door of the home.

"I love you, old man!" she gushed. "See you later! Have an awesome day today!"

Instantaneously, another recognizable voice from an unseen location within the home replied, "He will, honey. Just be careful, Danielle! We love you too."

From the front walk Dani bellowed out a response confirming she heard the voice, "I love both of you too!"

The voice Dani heard belonged to her mother, Vivienne. The beloved matriarch's facial expression conveyed appeasement. The soft but strong "North Star" guided the family in more ways than one. Her wisdom and love were needed and appreciated. She had just finished her morning run. She usually did three miles on the family treadmill every morning.

Franklin still stood in the kitchen nearby. Today anxiousness fueled Vivienne's greeting to her husband. She was full of energy. Adrenaline flowed through her sweaty body in high volume.

Entering into the L-shaped galley-like kitchen, she addressed her husband with much enthusiasm and sultriness. Vivienne tightly caressed Franklin from his backside.

"*Good morning, Mr. Mitchell.* How did my most prized possession sleep?" she purred. "This week is the big week!"

It was again that time of the year where quota requirements were nearing their meet date for the third quarter. Franklin had been diligently working to close a huge account in the process. He felt great about recent talks and negotiations, and was eagerly anticipating final adjustments for a close on his biggest client.

He had been working on this particular account since early last year. With too many vacillations to count, he finally felt more confident than ever about its completion.

“Yes, babe,” Franklin said with a smile. “This is the week, Viv. Lord knows it’s been a long race, but it’s nearing its end.

He pulled Vivienne’s hands from his chest, and placed them into his.

“I can see the flag man waving the checkered flag. It’s a huge week for us all babe. I just want so much to prove to Pop once and for all that I’m capable of the same big things he’s done and more.

“If everything goes well with Mr. Algieri and his team then I should be a shoo in to become the next firm partner. I can feel it. That’s so long as Mr. Maxwell or Pop doesn’t get in my way for that matter.”

“Frank, I’m proud of you,” Vivienne whispered. “Danielle, is proud of you, and as long as your family supports you then there is nothing else that matters.

“Just never let it consume you as it has your father. I’ve had plenty of conversations with your mother, and she longs for so many years she could have back with him. I don’t want that for us. Never for us!”

Vivienne turned her husband around and kissed him softly.

“Danielle’s last home game is in a couple of days,” she continued. “Let’s enjoy each other on that day as a family. I spoke with Lisa and she assured me that your planner was cleared on that evening months ago. So, I don’t want to hear any excuses.”

Franklin rubbed the back of his neck before responding to his wife, “Babe I can’t go.”

CHAPTER II

Don't let your mind speak louder than your heart.

"VIVIENNE, I CAN'T BAE. YOU'LL HAVE to cover for me," Franklin fussed. "With everything going on this week I'm just not sure that I'll be able to."

Vivienne's mouth twisted at his remarks. She had become visibly irritated. She didn't want to sound combative, but to hear Franklin say what he said disappointed her. She replied to his comments carefully.

"Franklin this is our daughter's last year in high school. You do know that right? Which means these are her last games she'll play at this level.

"You will be there because it means much more to us as a family than closing an account that only needs a signature. You have that account in the bag. I know it, and you know it! Nobody—not even the Maxwells can stop that deal from happening."

Vivienne leaned in closer. She kissed Franklin again softly.

"Go into the office this week, and do what you've always done, Franklin—get results. But do not miss Danielle's game! So, now if my dear husband will excuse me, I'm going to take a shower."

Vivienne drifted out of the room as swiftly as she had entered. Franklin grabbed his padded briefcase and the manila folder holding Mr. Algieri's files. He proceeded toward the front door blocking out what he had just heard from his wife. To him there was only one thing that was most important, and that was closing the account.

He'd closed huge accounts before, but this time it was different. This week meant accomplishing more than just a business deal, or receiving the perks for doing so. It meant solidifying his value at Mitchell, Leonard, and Maxwell. It meant finally proving to himself and to his father he could be what everyone said he wasn't capable of being.

The office was not more than a twenty-five-minute drive from the Mitchell home. It sometimes varied depending on the traffic. It was autumn in Georgia so the sun was radiant and bright. As its rays outstretched across all of the acreage lining the road, Franklin was put at ease about the account for a moment. His long-awaited sense of arrival was here now. Procuring a business relationship with Mr. Algieri meant procuring a partnership he always felt he deserved.

He continued to enjoy the scenery as his vehicle hugged each winding road of the rural countryside. Upon arriving into the city, he felt more eager and confident. Pulling closer to the American Art Deco style high rise of Mitchell, Leonard, and Maxwell, he felt meaningful for the first time in years.

The elevator ride up the building made of steel was a constant flow of stops and starts each day. It was eighteen floors both ways. Franklin usually started his day by placing important phone calls once he was in his office.

"Good morning, Lisa," he said brightly. "How was the game yesterday?"

Lisa Vega, Franklin's secretary, was in her late twenties, with high cheekbones, asymmetrical-shaped eyes, and golden bronze hair pulled back in a ponytail, she was the rambunctious omphalos of Franklin's professional life. She was standing between Franklin and his office door. It was as if she had anticipated his exact arrival into the office every day.

She handed him an itinerary with the day's date affixed at the top, "Good morning, Mr. Mitchell! The game was, oh gosh, it was fantastic! You should definitely see a live game! It was really something amazing."

"Oh, yeah? I think I may have to arrange that." Franklin replied.

He peered away from the itinerary to view Lisa displaying a huge smile that stretched to her ears.

"I mean…my trusted assistant may have to arrange it. I would love to see the Falcons play in their new stadium."

"Not a problem, Mr. Mitchell," Lisa declared.

"There are tons of home games left. But now that you are here, first things are first. You were scheduled to call Mrs. Fournier in ten minutes, but I already called her to reschedule the phone call."

"Why?" Franklin asked. "What did I miss?"

He adjusted his neck tie trying to physically convey he was prepared for anything. Lisa reached for Franklin's briefcase. It was a foretelling gesture.

"I rescheduled because your father wants to see you in his office," Lisa said.

Franklin's eyes darted toward the steel doors of the elevator.

"Did he mention what he wanted?" He asked.

"No, sir," Lisa replied. "Mrs. Rearden called, and she told me to tell you that he wanted to see you first thing this morning."

Mrs. Rearden was Arthur Mitchell's assistant. She had been with him for more than a decade.

"Okay, fine," he said apprehensively. "How do I look?"

"You're neat," Lisa teased.

"I'm neat?" Franklin asked in anguish. "Well then I guess this is bound to be an interesting morning."

Franklin stepped away toward the elevator. Mentally he had begun guessing what his father could possibly want. He could've called him personally, or left a message for Lisa. But if he wanted to see him then it must be serious.

Franklin never left his father's office over the years

without the short experience drastically changing his entire outlook on himself, his goals, or confidence.

Arriving on the twenty-third floor of the building, Franklin could suddenly feel all the eyes on the floor pierce toward him. He felt his internal temperature rise through his Dane Check jacket. He pretended not to notice as he loomed closer toward his dad's office.

The last time Franklin was on the twenty-third floor, he and Jacob Maxwell had a fifteen-minute war of words.

Jacob Maxwell was the son of senior partner Jacob Maxwell Sr. Although Jacob Junior despised the '*junior*' moniker, Franklin made sure to always address him as such. Franklin pushed onward. Mrs. Rearden's office was right outside his father's. They were conjoined rooms. He paced himself to neither appear late or too hasty.

"Has anyone seen one of the top twelve finalists from the nineteen seventy-four Miss Georgia Pageant?" he asked aloud.

He was speaking to a lady seated at a rustic macchiato desk. Mrs. Rearden looked up from her work over the top of her identical 'Billie Jean King' eyeglasses expressing thanks and a smile.

"Franklin, I can't even recognize that Ms. Veronica Rearden these days," she answered playfully. "That was so many years ago now. I was so young that I can't even remember what fashion was in."

Even with a face world weary, Mrs. Rearden still had the most angelic smile. Although her voice and body could appear feeble at times, she was still very much healthy at her age.

"How has my wonderful Franklin been?" She asked. "How are things with Vivienne and Dani?"

"They are fine," Franklin confirmed. "Everyone is active. How have y—"

"I didn't know you were a touristy guy Frank," a voice interrupted.

The voice projected behind him loudly. Franklin shook his head. With a clinched jaw he then finally turned around. Standing in the door of Mrs. Rearden's office was none other than Jacob Maxwell Jr.

With a mocking grin on his face he asked, "What? Were you a little bored downstairs?"

Franklin gathered himself.

A fake smile covered his face before he responded, "Yeah, Junior I was as a matter of fact. Sometimes whenever I'm bored, I just like to tour the building floor by floor to see the last name of my family engraved on all the walls."

Franklin inched forward to Junior almost close enough to be nose to nose.

He spoke up confidently and emphatically, "I tour these floors to bask in the fact that if it wasn't for my father Arthur Amos Franklin's purchase of your grandfather's failing company you might just be touring careerbuilder.com extensively and exclusively.

Junior's mouth curled upwards from his amusement.

"That's the thing Franklin," he said. "You're not your father, and you never will be."

CHAPTER III

Don't let your happiness be controlled by something you can't control.

AFTER A SHORT MOMENT OF AWKWARD silence, Mrs. Rearden spoke up and cut into the tension. "Franklin dear go on in, your father is ready to see you now."

Franklin turned away from his nemesis as angst had transformed both of their faces. He proceeded into his father's lush office space. The office was definitely a sight to see. Huge portraits of Franklin's grandfather and grandmother assisted with the décor. Along with various paintings and sculptures, Arthur made good use of the room's huge walls.

With all the plaques, the room maintained a cool motivational atmosphere. A massive European traditional style Grand Palais in the back left corner of the 550 square foot office covered a huge section of the space. In addition, there was also a long electric fireplace built into one of the walls that only added to the allure and mystique.

The room was magnificent to say the least. Franklin's father stood toward the back right side of the room. A statue could not have been more frozen in place. He stared intently out of a glazed tempered glass window.

"Son, what does sacrifice mean to you?" Arthur asked aloud.

He waited for a response. His eyes never left the Georgia skyline. It was a very beautiful autumn day, but somehow Arthur's words felt melancholic and ominous.

Although he was a little at a loss by the question, Franklin replied, "I believe it means giving up something you truly desire in order to achieve or receive something better in value."

Franklin paused. His nose wrinkled quicker than wool clothing.

"Pop, um, I apologize if I seem confused, but why do you ask?"

Arthur continued to stare through his office window.

He finally responded, "To so many people I'm simply Mr. Arthur, the Founder and Chief Executive Officer of Mitchell, Leonard, and Maxwell Partners.

"I direct investment strategies and decisions, firm governance, and investor relations. With more than fifteen billion in capital commitments and portfolio advisement that employs over five thousand employees worldwide. I have established a U.S. based investment firm with offices in Georgia, Florida, Illinois, and California that represent over sixty-seven billion dollars in transactional value."

Franklin was still no closer to any form of clarity than before Arthur began.

"Pop, isn't that what's on the company website? Your bio?" He carped. "Is something wrong? You sound like a Wikipedia page spewing out text word for word right now. Plus, I don't quite follow where you're going with all of this."

"Although I have tried to live simply, I understand that things are at best not all that simple. I must ask again. What does sacrifice mean to you, son?" Arthur asked.

"I just told you what I thought it meant. I literally just answered that quest—"

"Sacrifice is a catch-twenty-two, isn't it?" Arthur interrupted. "Look at my life. Along the way I've had to make many choices, same as everyone else. To some I am considered a trailblazer. For others it may be interpreted that I was at times foolhardy, but every decision took some sort of sacrifice for me.

"There have been choices I've made that I wish I could amend. I would amend them in such a way that appeasing my own self-interests wouldn't assume precedence. I say that only because some of those *foolhardy* choices made me an enemy of old friends.

"Those choices rewarded me with nothing more than the sycophantic and bloodthirsty alike. No one except maybe Lenny knew me better in this business."

Leonard "Lenny" Gordon, co-Founder of Mitchell,

Leonard, and Maxwell Partners, had always been a loyal and trusted friend of Arthur. Lenny had retired from the industry some time ago.

"Most times we sacrifice for many of the wrong reasons. Do you know what it is we sacrifice and waste the most?"

"Time maybe," Franklin answered nasally. "Look, pop what are you getting at? What is going on?"

"Time, precisely!" Arthur replied. "All the individual success and accolades don't mean anything if after you're gone, man or woman, you hadn't taken advantage of time. You can sacrifice many things in this lifetime, but sacrificing time should never be on the list."

"Can we get a timeout please?" Franklin begged. "Forgive me, but you're not making any sense! Plus, hopefully when I'm gone it's a long time from now!"

Arthur didn't even acknowledge Franklin's bafflement yet again.

He continued, "You know your mother has always been there every step of the way. Even when I wasn't the kindest or best person to be around.

"Your mother is the most beautiful, intelligent, caring, and thoughtful person I've ever known in my life. Yet, I sacrificed most of our time together. I sacrificed all of our time with each other for so many selfish endeavors. I should've been more supportive of you too.

You choosing NYU over U of C was so stupid a reason to hold a grudge against you. I wasted and sacrificed so many hours and moments I could've had with you both. All for what?"

Finally, Arthur started to move away from the

window. Franklin's eyes followed him as he walked around the room.

"Was it this Congressional Black Caucus Chair's Award on the wall here?" Arthur chides. "Maybe it was the Achievement Award over there. What about the Humanitarian of the Year Award or the Ripple of Hope Award? The Award of EXCELLENCE maybe? Better yet…that's what it is I bet! It could've been the U of C PROFESSIONAL ACIEVEMENT AWARD and Alumni Medal!!"

Arthur placed his hands into his pockets. He paused in the middle of the room before expelling an explosive noise that echoed high into the ceiling. He had begun coughing quite violently. The expulsion made him visibly wince at every repeating motion. The force shook him hard enough to alter his posture. He stumbled up against the east wall of his office for support.

"Pop?" Franklin pressed frantically. "Are you okay?!"

Arthur managed to compose himself. He swiped his hand in the air. He was motioning Franklin to keep back and remain where he was standing.

He turned away until with a beaded smile he continued, "I'm fine. Just a bit of dust in the room that's all. Um, where was I?"

He drew in a long breath.

"Oh, yes, in life there are times coming where you will have to make some very important choices. Life altering even! There will be a time when you may have to find the courage to sacrifice all the selfish vices and desires you may have for someone or something more important than your own self-interests. If decided correctly then you've got something no one can ever take away from you, and that is your soul.

"In the beginning I wanted to build this firm on principle. I had a true motivation to preserve the human experience. Especially the African-American experience. Individually I wanted to help them all. Help us as a people!

"That's what it was about, but I failed. In the beginning that was my, '*Why*'. But in the end my reasons changed. I tried hard to forget about the things I had done earlier on."

Franklin's thoughts swirled at this point. Every effort of coherency had failed. He walked toward his father in an attempt to give solace to a man seemingly out of sorts.

"Franklin, you have to be better than me," Arthur confided. "Whatever choices you are dealt to make in this life, understand they all have consequences no matter which way you spin the wheel."

"Pop, you have done great things!" Franklin assured. A sad smile overcame his features. "Sure, you sacrificed relationships and friendships, but you've helped a lot of people. Sure, those awards aren't anything but paper and gold patina. However, they are also symbols of your accomplishments. Right?"

The skin around Arthur's eyes bunched as he looked into Franklin's eyes. He then walked away from his son. He neared his desk to dial someone from the ancient looking telephone atop it.

"Send him in," he requested through the receiver.

He hung up the phone, and almost immediately a man walked in. He was in his mid-thirties, with a jet-black pompadour style haircut and build like a wide receiver. It was Junior. Chewing the inside of his mouth, Junior's Cheshire cat smile amplified Franklin's annoyance.

Franklin was even more confused now than he had been before. He gave Junior a stare so intense it was almost criminal. His chestnut irises dug into Junior.

"Good morning, Mr. Mitchell, sir!" Junior exploded with enthusiasm.

"Jacob, how are you?" Arthur replied.

Arthur took his seat as he gestured that both of his guests do the same. His office phone rang before he could begin to cut through the tension building inside the room.

"Yes?" he answered. "Okay, send him in."

The office door swung open. Walking into the huge office was another man Franklin was not fully fond of either, Jacob Maxwell, Sr. He was well beyond his first blush of youth, but still maintained a jaw line that would put Clark Kent to shame. Although muffled in his double-breasted suit, the sexagenarian was still a bit intimidating. Standing at six foot three, his uninviting disposition did not do much for approaching him at all.

"So, gentlemen I am rather late I see, nonetheless," Mr. Maxwell greeted. "Arthur, shall I?"

He glanced at Arthur, but proceeded without a response from him. Arthur rested his hands on the table as he directed his gaze back out of the office window.

"Franklin, as you know we are deeply appreciative of your work and the relationships you have established here at the firm. Especially, over the past few years," Mr. Maxwell started. "However, a change at this time we believe is needed to continue moving forward and growing this firm at an ideal pace."

"Okay, is anyone going to tell me what is going on, or should I hire an interpreter?" Franklin responded.

Franklin's flushed face showed signs of agitation. His eyes darted back and forth from his father to Mr. Maxwell.

"Well, for complete transparency, the Algieri account is of great importance to this firm," Mr. Maxwell affirmed. "It is also well-known at least amongst us that our business stands to make prominent strides if a business relationship of this magnitude is established and properly managed."

"I understand and I anticipate the deal will be done this week," Franklin disclosed.

Mr. Maxwell tilted his head sideways looking askance. Franklin forced a nervous laugh. The reason why he and the Maxwells were there started to dawn upon him. He was finally realizing what was occurring.

"Dad, what is this all about?!" Franklin burst out. "C'mon! I've busted my ass on this deal, and I can close it! I'm going to finalize this whole thing with Algieri. There is no doubt in my mind!"

"Well, frankly there is doubt, and unfortunately you won't be able to close the account," Mr. Maxwell mentioned.

"Why is that?" Franklin asked.

"As abrupt as it may be to you, effective immediately, we will be moving forward with my son Jacob on this account," Mr. Maxwell retorted. "It has already been done, and we feel confident he can close this deal right now rather than take any more chances with you on it.

"His background in engineering is not in contrast with Mr. Algieri's background like yours, and we feel it is better this way to finally reel him in."

Franklin tightly gripped the arms of his chair. Junior looked on with absolute enjoyment of Franklin's visible irritation.

"Well, I will be on my way if there is nothing more," Mr. Maxwell informed. "I have a flight to catch at noon, and I don't want to be late. Gentlemen good day…Arthur good day!"

Mr. Maxwell left the office more abrupt than he had entered. Junior's mocking smile could have lit up a cave. Franklin and Arthur were alone with him.

"I'll be sure to give Mr. Algieri your regards," Junior said. "All of your hard work on this account won't go unnoticed Frank. It may be necessary for an official introduction, but only if Mr. Mitchell thinks it's appropriate of course. I'll be sure to get all the files today as well. *ALWAYS BE CLOSING* right? Let Lisa know."

Junior finally left the room. Arthur's quietness filled Franklin with more contempt than he had ever felt for his father. He began to shake from the rush of anger and tumult.

"Is this why you called me up here today?!" He asked. "To sucker me in for what was about to happen?"

He continued as his emotions became clearly unstable, "You brought me up here to feed me all this bullshit about time and sacrifice just so you could slap me in the face yet again?! What do you want from me, huh?! What more do I have to prove to you?!

"Huh, Mr. CEO?! What??? Am I not as disruptive

as you were at my age? Am I a disappointment to you?!! Is that it? You were more successful right?!

"Not what you expected me to be, pop? No wait…that's not it! The University of Chicago, yeah, that's what it is! Didn't you say a moment ago that you should've been more supportive when I chose to go to NYU? That's it then, huh?!"

Franklin's disdain swelled over. Arthur never responded or took his gaze away from outside the office window during his son's entire emotional sequence.

"ANSWER ME DAMMIT!" Franklin boomed. "Is it because I don't have all these damn awards and plaques around my office as you do? Is that it?!

Franklin motioned to flip the chair he was seated in. Just as his fingers gripped the plush fabric, a loud voice echoed from across the room.

"FRANK!!!"

He recognized the voice, but the inflection was unfamiliar this time. He released his hold from the chair. His gaze fell to the floor. He turned his head to see none other than Mrs. Rearden standing inside the office by the door. She was the only other woman besides his wife and mother he believed could walk him away from a cliff's ledge if tempted. Exacerbated and anguished, Franklin's nostrils flared visibly. He inhaled deeply as his breathing was now heavy. He began to walk toward the beautiful solid hardwood door.

"Hear me and hear me good old man," Franklin ordered in a menacing tone. "You don't have to worry about any time you sacrificed to spend with me. I never needed your time nor is it welcomed now. Keep all your well wishes, and all other methods of your BULLSHIT!

You're dead to me. Just like you've always been!"

Franklin turned and walked out.

"No, Franklin wait," Mrs. Rearden pleaded. "Franklin, wait!"

Franklin hurried through the outside office as the wide eyes, gaped jaws, and raised eyebrows of other employees filled the room.

"Arthur, are you not going to stop him?" Mrs. Rearden asked. "Arthur?"

Arthur rose from his huge desk, and walked back over to his office window. He stood in the same place as he had earlier. Without a response, he continued his downcast gaze out at the Georgia skies.

CHAPTER IV

Be strong enough to let go.

Be patient enough to wait for what you deserve.

CERTAINLY THE MOST ORGANIZED PERSON within the offices of Mitchell, Leonard, and Maxwell had to be Lisa Vega. She is Franklin's executive assistant and number one handler. She knew everything there was to know about him. She also knew what it took to have him as prepared as possible. Lisa's military upbringing may have attributed to her certain scrupulous behaviors. She had been Franklin's admin for seven and a half years. Other than his wife and mother, nobody knew him better.

It was obvious to her before Franklin left the eighteenth floor that he probably wouldn't return as enthusiastically as he had left. She knew his relationship with his father was always on the tip of bubbling over. A few years ago, at a firm dinner party, Arthur publicly thanked Franklin's mother for not conceiving another child after he was born.

He stood up before the entire staff, guests, and members of Atlanta's business community and said jokingly, 'If I'd had a son who wanted it as much as I did when I was his age then maybe I could've retired ten years ago!'

The joke did not go over well with Franklin or his mother. Of course, Arthur stated he was joking, but the fact of the matter was that it embarrassed Franklin. It also began an unwarranted attachment of laziness to his name. It was another incident in the long history of an up and down father son relationship. Those words lit a fire under Franklin though. The Algieri account was just what he needed to catapult him into the laurels of the distinguished advisors within the firm.

It had been a little bit over two hours since Lisa had seen Franklin, and still no word from him.

'*The meeting couldn't have lasted this long, could it?*' Lisa thought to herself.

She picked up the telephone to place a call to Mrs. Rearden. Instead of a dial tone she heard a voice on the other end of the receiver.

"Hello," the voice said.

"Hello?" Lisa replied.

"'Lisa, is this you?" the voice asked.

"Yes, this is Lisa," Lisa confirmed. "Mr. Mitchell?"

"Yes, it's me, Lisa," Franklin said hurriedly. "I've left the office, and I need you to get the Algieri file together for me. Have it ready to transfer over to either Junior or his assistant. Change out its folder also. Thank you."

"Mr. Mitchell, I don't understand," Lisa informed. "So, you want me to give the entire Algieri file and its documents to Mr. Maxwell Jr.?"

"Yes!" Franklin affirmed.

There was an awkward silence. Lisa could hear Franklin inhale deeply. Yelling at her was neither something she concerned herself with or took personally. She could sense he was clearly upset about something.

"Is everything okay, sir?" she asked quietly.

To convey contrition Franklin went on, "Lisa, I'm sorry for that just now. I'm a little bit on edge. However, it doesn't justify me yelling at you because of it. Forgive my frustration, please."

"I understand, Mr. Mitchell," Lisa assured. "No, need for apologies. But you are forgiven if that helps. So, I take it you will be out of office for the rest of the day?"

"Yes, lock up my office, hold all my calls, and clear today's schedule," Franklin said. "I won't be back in till tomorrow maybe."

"Okay, I will do it," Lisa pledged. "So, I will give the Algieri account files to Mr. Maxwell Jr. effective immediately. Anything else? Oh, what about your briefcase?"

"Put it inside my desk," Franklin replied. "Keep all points of contact open in case I need something else. Thank-you, Lisa. I don't know what I'd do without you."

"Well, thanks sir, and I'm not leaving," Lisa chorused. "By the way don't forget your schedule is clear for Danielle's game this week also. Be safe, Mr. Mitchell. Bye-Bye."

A few hours passed by after Lisa spoke to Franklin. Preparing the file for a transfer probably could've been done a lot quicker, but her attention to detail outweighed any proclivity she may have had for carelessness.

'Lunch can wait a few more minutes.' She said to herself.

Finally, after another half hour, Lisa had the account file, relationship notes, and financial documents together. Once everything was done, there were three folders of paperwork.

Inside the amber folders were salesforce notes, unsigned written agreements, recent business decisions, and bios of everyone of any importance involved with the Algieri business. Everything was all ready and waiting to be handed over.

After gathering her belongings to step out for lunch, Lisa decided to place a call to Junior's assistant. As the line rung, Lisa peered outward over the half empty office floor. She then recognized the most talked about and famed pompadour hairstyle of the building. Maxwell Jr. was stepping out of the elevator.

He inched forward. His eyes were already narrowed and turned up. His mouth made Lisa's smile fade from her face. She cringed slightly. At the same time, a voice, soft spoken and light-hearted, finally could be heard through the receiver. It was Junior's assistant.

"Hi, it's Lisa Vega calling on behalf of Mr.

Franklin Mitchell for Mr. Maxwell," Lisa started. "Never mind though. Mr. Maxwell is on our floor now. I'll speak to him directly. Thanks."

Lisa hung up the phone to greet Junior. By now he was standing right in front of her.

"It's been quite a while, Lisa," Junior said.

"It has been, Mr. Maxwell," Lisa replied.

"C'mon, why are you being so formal?" he said. "What happened to calling me, Jacob? It's not like you haven't before. Where's, Frankie?"

With her eyebrows arched and wrinkled nose showing signs of her mood, Lisa found a small amount of politeness to acknowledge Junior's question, "*Mr. Mitchell* stepped away from the office to attend a previous engagement across town. He won't be back for quite some time."

Maintaining eye contact, he continued, "Hmm, so ole Frankie stepped out, huh? It should have been expected. He isn't one to run, but it's understandable why he would now.

"Once he found out he was replaced on the Algieri account I figured he wouldn't know how to handle it. All along I thought my father was behind the idea but no! Boy was I wrong. His own father did it! Those Mitchells sure are a messy bunch, aren't they?"

Junior's mocking of Franklin only made Lisa more annoyed and eager to remove herself from his presence. He moistened his lips very slowly and methodically as he continued.

"You know once I make partner if you're interested you can come aboard as my executive admin. With all of the business coming my way I know I'll need to hire someone to cover all the extra work. It will pay very well of course. Much more than your current salary!"

"*Partner*?" Lisa questioned nasally.

"Yes, p*artner!*" Junior declared. "You see once I close the Algieri account then that will be enough to transcend my status here at Maxwell, Leonard &…. I mean Mitchell, Leonard, and Maxwell."

Junior found great pleasure in mocking the Mitchells. It satisfied him to such a degree that he chuckled at himself almost unconsciously. His display of arrogance and self-absorption further exacerbated Lisa's displeasure.

"You do mean limited partner don't you, Junior?" she asked. "Oh, I'm sorry. I know how much you hate that name. Apologies."

Lisa corrected herself, "I meant to say *Jacob*."

Junior forced a brash laugh. He then aggressively snatched the Algieri files from her desk.

"You know Mr. Algieri and his IPSOS Corporation are the future of tech," he proclaimed. "But I wonder what took Frankie so long to know that.

"You should also be aware by now that the fact of the matter is that your boss is not good at what he tries to do. I mean does your Frank ever take anything other than his dad's opinion seriously?

"Tech—it's the future! You know what else? *I'M THE FUTURE*! I'm the future of this firm and of my family! Once this deal is closed, I think you may want to reconsider my offer. Oh, and I have to ask you something because I've been wondering. Do you still keep all your cute little socks in the double dresser by your bed?"

Lisa's eyes roll almost out of their sockets, "Is that all, Junior?"

"Yeah, for now," Junior chirped. "I'll catch you around eventually, *Ms. Vega*."

Junior turned and walked back toward the elevator to leave. Over his shoulder he taunted, "Better yet maybe not. It's more than likely I'll be too busy to care anymore."

CHAPTER V

Pain is inevitable. Suffering is optional.

ON THE OTHER SIDE OF TOWN IT WAS THE same business as usual for Dani. She was primed up for this year's volleyball tournament and graduation. Standing at her locker, filled with books and posters of the latest musical talents, she prepared for her first class. It was her final year in high school, and it meant a lot to her personally to embrace it fully and finish strong. Although the 'Lady Jayhawks' had already secured a playoff berth in the tournament, she was determined to have an epic final home game. It was all about the experiences and moments that came with the memories. She had always been heavily involved with volleyball and track.

Her love for the two sports started when she was a little girl. She idolized her mother Vivienne for her athletic abilities. Vivienne was a former high school champion and standout sprinter for four straight years. Dani was a terror to opponents just like her mom was. Opposing runners very seldom stood a chance at exhibition track meets. With her athleticism, training, and preparation, Dani excelled tremendously at both sports for years.

St. Lucas finished their season last year by winning the state championship. Capturing the title for their second year in a row. This year she and her teammates were going for three consecutive gold trophies. The team would be the only other team to do so since George Walton High School, a rival, did so back in 2013.

"Is your family coming to the game Dani?" A lively voice asked.

It wasn't unusual for that specific person to be as excited as she was at that time of day.

Before closing her locker Dani responded with a simple, "Yes."

She recognized the jovial voice even though her locker door blocked the person's face. As she closed the dull blue colored steel locker door, two of her closest friends were standing near her. Both ladies had wide grins that showed all thirty-two teeth. One of them, Monica, stood five foot eight inches with glossy skin. She started fumbling around inside her purse that was looped over her shoulder.

She was the track and field team's power runner. She had just about the same moxie as any amateur prizefighter. Running in the last position during relay races allowed her to demonstrate her fierce competitiveness time and time again.

"I can't find my freaking lip gloss anywhere," she confessed.

Although she was more often a cheerful and organized character, today she was out of sorts. She was preoccupied with digging through the miniature tote she had. Being St. Lucas' co-captain on the track and field team required discipline and resolve, but at the moment you wouldn't be able to tell she had any.

Dani's other friend, Emma, was the cheerful and lively one. With a set of dazzling, angel-white teeth, she peered in Dani's direction with her eyes crossed and fat smile. With her jet-black hair and slender eyebrows, she was another five-foot seven-inch powerhouse for the track and field and volleyball teams.

Both of Dani's friends had just turned eighteen and had sculpted figures from their similar training regimes. It wasn't uncommon for the ladies to stay conditioned during the off season. Along with Dani, both of them had recently procured scholarships to play collegiate sports next season.

"So, I see one of you is in a happy mood," Dani joked. "Why the clown face today, Emma? What's the occasion?"

"Because it's finally here," Emma replied. "It's tournament time! It's state championship three years in a row time! It is finally about to be wild college party time!!"

Monica's eyes nearly rolled out of their sockets.

"So, I guess that means the stars are finally aligned huh?" Monica croaked.

"Um, excuse me!" Emma effused. "You two are

such Debbie Downers."

All three ladies laughed as they started their way down the hallway away from Dani's locker.

"So, which of our parents will be attending the final home game besides mine?" Dani asked.

"*Besides yours*?" Monica mocked. "*Yeah, okay.* Sure, they'll be there!"

"Whatever," Dani replied.

"Well, my mother will be in Colorado for work again, but my dad should be there," Monica continued. "Dad has and will always support me the way my mother never can or ever tried to. She won't ever get it. She's still pushing for me to follow in her footsteps. Business this and business that.

"Since graduation is finally here, I've been doing some serious thinking you know. I know I was able to get a scholarship to USC, but sometimes I wonder what if I get there, and I'm not the next Allyson Felix as all these scouts project me to be.

"My dearest mother sure thinks I won't be the next Allyson Felix. She's such a negative person. If she's correct though then what happens?"

Trying to encourage her friend, Emma burst out, "Monica you worry too much girl! We should be living the time of our lives right about now! Stop worrying.

"You won't be the next Allyson Felix, but you will be the first and only *MONICA KINSLEY*! Oh, and by the way the two of us will definitely be there for you girl! Old pal!! Old friend!!"

Emma laughed out loud as the three continued

down the school corridor.

"Besides, we all have parent issues," Emma admitted. "My parents said they'll be in attendance with the two little brats, but what else is new though right? I want you both to know something since this seems to be sharing time and all. It doesn't mean anything just because my parents show up that they support me more than either of yours."

Monica gave Emma a blank stare before continuing to dig in her purse for her missing cosmetic.

"To clarify I feel like now since I'm eighteen I'm just someone sleeping in their house," Emma uttered. "Now the brats?! Oh, yeah, they're the ones who get all the attention these days. DEFINITELY NOT I. Do not be fooled by the misconception that just because my parents are there that they are truly *there*."

"As if you weren't ever one of those spoiled brats you called siblings," Dani said heartily.

Emma acknowledged the truth in Dani's assessment by nudging her in the arm.

"Well, my dad said he's going to be here for the game!" Dani uttered. "At least he better be! For once Lord can he show up for anything besides his client meetings? It would mean so much to win the last home game while he's there too. For me it would mean a little bit more, win or lose if both Mrs. Vivienne and Mr. Frank were in attendance. But who knows?"

Finally, the ladies made it to their class. They paused in the corridor before going in. Dani's eyes froze open. She couldn't hide her sudden dismay.

"UGH!" Monica grunted. "I just bought this lip

gloss. Did I let either one of you borrow it?"

Monica continued to dig around in the tote as if it would reveal itself after more searching.

"It will definitely be an emotional day for me," Dani continued. "I mean to know we will all be in a different environment and away from each other soon is tough to wrap my mind around.

"You both are my girls, and I care for you both dearly. I know things will change, but I don't want them to change so drastically. Tell me you guys feel it too!"

"*Aww,* Danielle that is so sweet," Emma chorused. "I think the tears may start to fall even earlier than ex—"

"Anyway!" Monica interjected "Dani you're the one with the most heart amongst all three of us. You deal with situations way better than we both do.

"I thought I'd never see the day you get all mushy on us. All I've ever seen you do is focus on your grades, and who you're going to beat on the field next."

"Since I was *so* rudely interrupted!" Emma shouts. "If I can be real though, we never have seen you focus on anything else Dani. Monica is right. It's like you're always zoned in. Never too high. Never too low. So, yeah, don't go getting all sappy now!"

The young girls chuckled at one another.

Emma leaned in closer, "Group hug!!"

All three girls embraced. They had all known each other since elementary school. They wouldn't let attending different college campuses after graduation change the pact that formed amongst the three.

"I care deeply about the both of you too!" Dani said affectionately. "I recognize both of you as my sisters for life! You both know this. That's why it's getting more difficult for me as the semester flies by.

"That's all, but I'm okay now. Lord willing, we don't let anything come between us. Let's keep our relationships solid! Never let it end up like the ones we have with our parents. Deal?"

"DEAL!" all the girls chorused.

CHAPTER VI

Know my mind, and you'll know my heart.

"LET ME ASK YOU SOMETHING THOUGH. Is Mr. Mitchell really coming?" Monica asked. "I know the final game will mean much more to you if he shows. We just need your head in the right space. All the girls need you at your best come tournament time."

"Monica?" Emma fussed. "Drop it okay. jeez!"

"I just don't want Dani to be disappointed or out of her element on game day if he doesn't show," Monica confessed. "How many times has he said in the past ten years he'll be there and he never showed?

“Since I’ve known you? How many times has he bought you off with presents and cards? It’s sort of like my mother does me! I mean you are tough as nails, but how much can you take Captain Marvel? You have to confront him.”

“Oh, like you’ve done your mom?” Emma sassed.

“Whatever, Emma!” Monica countered. “Your parents are the Cosby’s compared to ours! Dani, all I’m saying is one game won’t change all the years he’s missed sharing moments with you in the past. I—”

“He’ll be at the game!” Emma vowed. “He will! Monica, get off it!”

By the time Emma finished speaking Dani had drifted away from the ladies’ conversation deep into her own thoughts. It was if Monica’s words caused a chain reaction of moments and memories Dani had suppressed only to have reawakened.

Memories of all the times Franklin fell short of keeping his word. She remembered all the times he had to make up a broken promise with presents instead of his presence.

Both Emma and Monica stared at their friend. Their half-lidded eyes watched as Dani’s mind drifted someplace else.

“Dani?” Emma teased.

Danielle didn’t respond.

“DANI!!” Monica yelped.

Dani fumbled out of her daze,

“Huh?! My bad. What did you ask me? Yeah, my

dad will be there with my mom. He doesn't have any plans so he will be there this time. He confirmed with me this morning."

With raised eyebrows and a wrinkled brow, Monica's expression summarized her lack of confidence in Dani's statement. Emma and Dani both noticed her features.

"What Monica?!" Dani asked. "What do you want me to say? He's going to be there, and even if he isn't then *oh well.* He won't affect my play if he doesn't show. I'll be focused going into the tourney. Trust me!"

Monica took her attention from the ladies and looked down the hall. With her eyes squinted, she peered toward the exit doors in the distance.

"What are you staring at?" Emma asked. "What happened?"

"Well, I thought I saw Dani's dad showing up for once," Monica scoffed. "Oh, my mistake. It's not him. That's just the janitor."

"You're not right," Dani quipped. "He'll be here! Maybe he's not the perfect dad, but he's mine. I bet I know who won't be here though!"

The school bell interrupted the three young ladies. The bell was a signal that it was a quarter past eleven and time for third period. Mr. Henderson's class was next. It was a fun class except for when you were late.

The ladies raced to class. Once inside and at her seat, Dani's thoughts raced around Monica's comments from moments ago. It's as if she couldn't expel Monica's inquiries from her mind.

'*Monica was just a concerned friend and sister. It's*

not like she wasn't stating the obvious.' Dani thought to herself.

For those reasons, Dani couldn't fault her. If so, then it still would be misdirected. If no one else understood what she was feeling then Monica definitely did.

Monica's relationship with her mother was as complicated if not more complicated than Dani's relationship with her father. There were too many instances to validate both of the young ladies' frustrations.

Franklin and Monica's mother were notorious for not keeping their word. Although Dani never confronted her father about how she felt, his absences had insurmountable effects on her. She found ways to dismiss and suppress them over time.

The last home game was symbolic for more reasons than the obvious ones. It was a celebration of her teammates, and the culmination of an unbelievable journey at St. Lucas. Some of those same people she had known for three or more years were at their final chapter too. It meant the end of something special she shared with each one. It meant the beginning of something foreign not yet seen or understood.

She would be leaving the comforts of her home soon. She would be leaving the beautiful Georgia mountain tops that pierced the unbounded sky for an environment contrary to it all. She was seeking assurance that her relationship with Franklin was not headed down the same road her grandfather's relationship with her father was.

'Could she ever be able to trust her father's word at all?' She thought to herself.

Dani wanted Monica's insinuations to be proven

wrong. She hated the fact that what she proclaimed was true. It was a difficult feeling to describe in words. Anxiety played a game of tug of war in her abdomen just thinking of all the things she would miss once she was away.

Outwardly, Dani maintained her dimpled smile and jovial attitude. It was so admired amongst everyone she knew. She was a mentor to a few freshmen students and others around campus. Yet, inwardly she couldn't quite put her finger on why she never dealt with how she's felt over the years.

She dedicated herself to honing her skills and talents to be one of the top athletes in the state. Yet, in so many ways she never made time to deal with anything else other than school and sports. It took an extreme focus to maintain a three-point eight grade point average. All the while participating in extracurricular activities at her level. Maybe Monica was right. Dani kept replaying it all in her mind.

'What if a conversation is something I should have before leaving? Am I mentally ready to hear what he might say? What if I'm not as good as the scouts believe I am on the collegiate level? Is this really what I want to do, or am I doing what my mother wants? What about my relationship with my parents? How will things change? Will they remain the same?' She thought more.

Dani's mind was clearly not indulged or engaged in class. However, Mr. Henderson churned out another lecture. She was usually his go-to student in each class. Most times the rest of her peers were either spaced-out or completely off-kilter from the class lecture.

Once class was almost over, Mr. Henderson called out to her, "Dani please by all means answer this question for the rest of the class. What makes Michael Porter's Five

Force Analysis prevalent in today's business world?"

Deep in a daydream, Dani was completely off grid within her thoughts.

"Dani?" he called out again.

Monica suddenly pressed the pointed end of her pencil into Dani's back. A sharp pain radiated throughout her body, but it jolted her out of her stupor, Dani replied before Mr. Henderson could call out to her a third time.

"Oh, um, Mr. Henderson, can you repeat the question?" she asked. "I didn't quite understand what you asked."

"Okay Dani," he complied. "Why is Michael Porter's Five Force Analysis still widely pre—"

Dani fired back a quick answer to his question, "It analyzes competition in t—"

Suddenly, the shrill sound of the school bell interjected whatever thought she had. It rattled throughout the entire campus. Any effort for a complete reply was over.

"Okay, students that's it for today," Mr. Henderson guaranteed. "Remember to live full and live intently. Maturity of the mind is the capacity to endure all uncertainty."

Mr. Henderson motioned back toward his desk after watching a few students pile out of his classroom. Dani tried her best to blend in with the last of the crowd, but Mr. Henderson noticed her.

He glanced up from the moderately organized stacks of white papers atop his modest desk.

"Dani, can you come here for a second?" he asked.

Dani's ears turned scarlet as she responded, "Sure, Mr. Henderson. What's on your mind?"

CHAPTER VII

Sometimes you just need a break, alone,
in a beautiful place to figure things out.

MONICA AND EMMA REMAINED IN THE doorway as if they had invisible cloaks on. Mr. Henderson glanced toward the two restive young ladies as they waited in the entrance of the classroom.

His distinct chuckle filled the room before he addressed them both, "Ladies, is it okay if I have a moment with Danielle?"

"Sure," Emma said with a bubbly smile. "Sorry, Mr. Henderson. We weren't trying to eavesdrop. We'll be right outside, Dani."

"Thank you, ladies," he replied.

The girls walked away from the door, but not too far down the hallway. Monica made a gesture to Emma to walk back closer to the doorway in an attempt to eavesdrop. They could hear Mr. Henderson's voice but couldn't comprehend what exactly he was saying. Although he had a powerful voice, he was speaking softly.

"So, Dani, I noticed you were a bit removed from class today," Mr. Henderson expressed. "That's quite unusual for you. Normally you are so engaged. Is everything, okay? I understand the district tournament is about to begin so I promise I won't make the Mid-Term too difficult for you guys."

The glowing appreciation on Dani's face shone brighter than the sun. She was gratified that Mr. Henderson was concerned. It showed someone other than her friends cared about what was going on with her. But it also gave insight to the fact that her emotions might be more visible than she wanted them to be. Mr. Henderson recognized it right off. She respected the fact he was still the same mentor she had grown to laud and admire.

"Thanks, Mr. Henderson," she said. "But I'm fine. It's not that."

Exhaling all of the built-up oxygen within her diaphragm caused her to pause. She looked down at the floor.

"Well, do you want to talk about it?" Mr. Henderson asked with more concern.

Hesitation engulfed Dani as she peered away from Mr. Henderson. She wondered if it even mattered to mention what was on her mind as she stared out through the condensed panes of the classroom. The sun was gleaming over the Georgia sky. Dani wondered was it even something worth addressing seriously.

"Mr. Henderson," she said. "I keep asking myself if I'm ready for the things that are about to change. Some things are changing already."

"Okay," Mr. Henderson responded. "Like what? Are you questioning your preparation in response to those changes?"

"Sort of I would say," she said. "I've been asking myself what if I lose interest in running. What if I lose interest in participating in any of the things I've had to do to get my scholarship? Then what? What even happens over time to all the things that never change, but you wish they would?"

"Meaning?" Mr. Henderson asked.

"Relationships," Dani charged. "Like what happens to relationships or friendships over time? You know like the ones you cherish, but know they are not as strong as they could be. Those that need the change."

"What if the foundation of those relationships isn't as pristine or infallible, but opaquer? I'm sorry Mr. Henderson. I'm rambling. It's just my thoughts are buzzing about that's all."

"No, it's fine Dani," Mr. Henderson assured. "I think I may understand a bit better if I knew the context of your troubles better."

"Well," Dani started. "It just so happens that someone implied if I don't deal with certain issues of my past, then I wouldn't be able to move forward. It somewhat made me feel vulnerable to the point of it breaking my invincible superhero shield everyone believes I have.

"Although most students think so, I'm not a superhero, Mr. Henderson. Sure, there are things I haven't dealt with internally, but other things needed my focus. Now I wish I would've dealt with things way back when—things that troubled me."

"Dani, you are a wonderful student, person, and inspiration to a lot of your peers here," Mr. Henderson said proudly. "St. Lucas appreciates it and thrives because of students like you. As your teacher I will even say you are an inspiration for teachers such as myself.

"You are a superhero that has extraordinary powers! You are admired by so many. Yet I do believe internally and externally everyone has to eventually face what's bothering them. Not to sound cliché here, but truly '*face their fears*'. Only because it's a way to fully recognize, address, and forgive yourself.

"It's also a way to fully address anybody that has transgressed against you as well. I would guess that whatever you're holding on to is not as bad as it seems in the sense that it was necessary to build you up.

"However, holding on to it or sweeping it under a rug rather than dealing with it has its way of making you address it. The past has a funny way of fueling motivation! It can also add to the disappointment, emotional, and/or mental stress too. But only if you let it.

"So, dealing with whatever is causing these questions to formulate I would say is necessary. Free yourself from those things having control over you. Because in the end I believe the number one goal is to be happy.

"Before you go, I will tell you a story. For such a long time I have held away all the things I felt about never knowing my biological mother. The emptiness and feeling of being rejected was something I thought I could fill or suppress with my work and other things.

"But truthfully it was a burden on my own family. My biological mother left my father when I was very young. So, I grew up believing my stepmother was my real mother. Although she isn't, I still consider her my biological mother. I remember finding out my freshmen year in high school that she wasn't."

"How did you feel?" Dani asked.

"Truthfully, it left me feeling deceived and unsure of what other things were hid from me. Unfortunately, my pride and fear kept me from ever locating my real mother for quite some time. After realizing I didn't want to carry that weight any longer or allow the anger to fester, I sought her out. I needed that meeting. I waited until I was 39 before I stopped kidding myself.

"It was brief but for my own closure it saved years of my life. I didn't want to be guessing or questioning myself '*What if?*' for the rest of my days. As much as she didn't want to face me, I believe till this day that I am better for it."

Mr. Henderson's words resonated with Dani. She had begun to relax knowing that one of her biggest influences had gone through something similar.

"It makes a lot of sense, Mr. Henderson," she said. "Everything you just said was very impactful. Thank you for your story, and entrusting me with it also."

"No, problem," replied Mr. Henderson. "Hey, it could have come from anywhere, but today I was just the conduit to deliver it. Remember that sometimes you don't have to look too far to find what you seek.

"Sometimes the most important answers are right in front of us. So, no need to thank me. Hopefully, it helps you answer the questions you may have. See you tomorrow?"

By this time Mr. Henderson's next class of students had entered the room for his fourth period lecture.

With a dimpled smile lighting up her face Dani responded, "I'll see you tomorrow!"

She exited the room.

"Danielle!!!" Monica and Emma screeched in unison.

Dani's two young friends shouted out for her attention as she appeared in the corridor. They retreated into the girl's bathroom once they realized how loud they had been. Dani walked down to the end of the hall where the bathroom was located. Her furrowed brow was too visible to hide.

She smiled softly as she entered the bathroom. Monica and Emma stood in the room touching up their lips and hair. The lavatory resembled a 4-star hotel lavatory and not one consistent with a bathroom inside a typical high school filled with blithely unconcerned teenagers.

"Emma, you have my lip gloss!" Monica said impatiently.

She shifted her weight from one foot to the other.

She continued. "I remember now! I asked you to hold it yesterday, or was that you, Dani?"

Monica was clearly unsure. Annoyed by her current interrogation, Emma brushed her comments off.

"*Anyway,*" Emma hissed.

Emma returned her sight to Dani. With her eyebrows elevated, she nudged and asked, "So, what did Mr. Henderson want?"

"Nothing really," Dani offered. All I can say is that Mr. Henderson is what I will miss about St. Lucas. He still stands out as one of my favorite teachers. He said some very profound things I'll definitely adhere to. As always of course, but he also said 'Sometimes you don't have to look very far to find what you seek'."

Then in a perfect sequence Dani reached into her purse and pulled out Monica's misplaced lip gloss. Emma and Dani both laughed in chorus together at Monica. Monica's eyes grew wide as she uncrossed her arms. She snatched the cosmetic away from Dani. With her own distinguished giggle, she joined in with the laughter. Once the three ladies finally exited the bathroom their laughter filled the garish hallways all the way to class.

CHAPTER VIII

If you want to talk, just come. Anytime. Anywhere.

FRANKLIN PULLED PAST THE RED MAPLE trees lined along a winding road. His irritation was still at a high point. The beautiful rays of the sun peering through the scarlet draped foliage of his parent's neighborhood was always a sight to see. Especially at that time of year. However, the massive trees in all of their glory could not overtake Franklin's emotions. He was overwrought with agitation and exhausted with anger.

'How could he do this to me? 'Do I know what sacrifice is?' Oh, I sure don't know what sacrifice is! Not after I've worked my ass off day in and day out!' He thought to himself.

No topical or secret elixir could remedy his pain. As he finally reached the wrought iron gate of his parent's property, he exhaled deeply. It was the undeniable sound of a near defeated man. Once inside the gate, Franklin saw a familiar car parked out in front of the enormous home.

It appeared to be Vivienne's sedan. Franklin parked his vehicle. He took a moment before going exiting. The woman he knew he wanted to share his grief with was waiting inside to share her exceptional wisdom. Even so, he needed a moment to decompress. Plus, the woman he depended upon for so much support was inside with her. Perfect timing on his part. At this moment he needed them both.

Franklin got out. He pressed his face within his palms as he leaned up against his metallic grey vehicle. The Oak wood door of the house began to open just as he had gathered himself. He slowly walked toward the front walkway of the home. Emerging from within his parent's home was a middle-aged man, with storm-grey hair, cerulean blue eyes, and a welcoming smile. His suspenders and checkered dress shirt hugged his clean-limbed anatomy. He walked toward the car Franklin assumed was Vivienne's.

The gentleman glanced over at Franklin and cheerfully addressed him, "Hi, there! Beautiful day to be alive, isn't it?"

He smiled at Franklin with all of the muscles in his face. The man's apparent appreciation of life and sheer glee didn't steer Franklin's irritation away any. The sedan the gentleman had was the same make, same model, same color, same tint, and same everything Vivienne's sedan was.

'Who the hell is this?' A befuddled Franklin thought to himself.

The gentleman took his tailored Havana double breasted jacket he was holding and placed it on the backseat of the luxury car. Finally, he hopped into the vehicle and slowly pulled away.

Franklin took his gaze away from the departing vehicle's license plate and entered the house. The custom-built Mediterranean home exuded a relaxed sophistication. With its multiple porches and structure, it was a magnificent edifice to witness. The formal living room and dining areas flanked the front entry with towering ceilings.

Franklin made his way deeper into the home. Passing by the study and open staircase, he entered the family room that opened into the custom kitchen. It too was also a beauty to behold. It maintained marble counter tops and a massive island.

Standing at one of the counters was Franklin's mother, Denise Ann Mitchell. She was just the person who he had called off the rest of his day for. She was the other parent he wanted and needed to see. Denise didn't even notice Franklin had entered into the house. She was too busy pruning a vase full of flowers. Franklin had always kept keys to the home anyway.

"Chrysanthemums this fall, huh?" Franklin asked.

He was serving notice of his presence more so than inquiry. Denise was known throughout the city for her "Garden Club" and love for flowers. She was somewhat of a savant when the discussion was flowers.

Over her shoulder Denise replied, "That has to be my son."

She turned to see Franklin's lopsided smile.

"Honey, it's so good to see you!" Denise declared. "I didn't hear you come in. Did you miss your mother?"

"Well, of course," Franklin agreed. "Always! But I came by to see you and to vent."

"Tell me," Denise said. "What's new?"

"Well, a list of unexpected events, but then again that's not new," Franklin groaned.

Denise started back fidgeting with her Chrysanthemums.

She peeked up from her activity on the island, "I'm sorry to hear you had a rough day, Frank. Anything out of the ordinary?"

Franklin forced a laugh. He was trying his best not to alarm her.

"Nothing different I guess," he lied. "How are you feeling, though? Well, before you answer, who was that man that just left?"

"Who, Daniel?" Denise asked. "He has business with your father. Don't you remember him? He's certainly grown up to be quite the businessman.

"He oversees Arthur's business affairs and the estate. Daniel took over for his father after his passing. Now the family business is all his. Don't you remember Mr. Gideon? *Charles Gideon*?

"He was always over for dinner parties when you were younger. He had a very distinctive belly laugh and an invigorating demeanor. If you can remember the clouds of cigar smoke then you can remember Charles, I'm sure. He and the clouds of smoke were never too far apart."

Franklin's brow raised as he recollected.

"Until you mentioned cigars, I had no clue of who you were referring to," Franklin confirmed. "I think I remember him now though. He asked me to call him Charlie instead of Mr. Gideon.

"When I would see him that's what he would ask me to call him. He was always very nice to me whenever you or dad would have me keep the guests entertained with my magic routines. You're right, he was never too far from a thick trail of smoke."

Franklin chuckled to himself as he had rediscovered memories of the man. He remembered the map of wrinkles covering his face.

"Wow, I can't believe I forgot about Mr. Charlie," Franklin brayed. "I never knew he had passed away though. Here today and gone today, I guess. Isn't that how it works?"

A blank stare transformed Franklin's face as he settled back into his previous disposition. Now he was back to resembling a man in bereavement than a man delighted by childhood memories. Exasperated and dejected, his thoughts of Mr. Charlie brought a brief reprieve from his horrid day, but it didn't last long. If it were said that he was anything other than tense it would be a false description.

Cognizant of the atmosphere, Denise's attention had long left her Chrysanthemums. Gazing at Franklin, she sensed his lowly energy. It certainly wasn't the demeanor of someone about to sure-up the biggest deal in his career.

Franklin's empty stare was plastered in place and

his posture was telling. Denise eyed his plodding movements. If someone were to blow on him, he would fall right over.

"Frank, tell me what happened." Denise ordered. "You look really exhausted. Are the girls, okay? Is everything going well with the Algieri account?"

The muscles around Franklin's mouth tensed.

"Is Pop feeling, okay?" he asked. "Has everything been okay with him lately?"

Denise showed a half-hearted smile. She turned away to minimize eye contact.

Over her shoulder she responded again, "He's fine. Why do you ask since you won't answer my question?"

"It doesn't matter I guess," he charged. "Pop is always going to be who he is. Our relationship at this point will never be more than what it is. It's certainly undefinable to me now, and believe it or not it has been for a while. I'm not willing to try anymore or anything else to salvage it now!

"He isn't the man I revered back when I was a high strung eight-year-old kid. He isn't that man anymore. I'm not willing to overextend my efforts for him or the firm anymore either! It's to a point now where I can't look at him, Mom.

"How does that happen?! Seriously, I'm at a crossroads, and I'm thinking about leaving the firm. It may be the best thing to do at this point. I can start my own Fund like I've been saying and wanting to do forever. I just can't keep wasting my time and energy trying to fix something I didn't break."

"So, what happened with you and your father

today?" Denise asked. "Aren't you going to tell me? What disaster made you drive all the way here through city traffic rather than to call?"

Franklin's nose flared. Then anger crossed his face.

"So, I made it to the office this morning and Lisa told me Pop wanted to see me," Franklin responded. "The first thing he asked me was 'What does sacrifice mean to me?' I thought it was rhetorical at first, but he truly wanted an answer from me. Of course, my answer was too general for him.

"Then he proceeds to tell me that I no longer have the Algieri account. Afterwards, to make matters worse—your husband gave the account to Junior! Out of all the advisors there! Thinking back on it now, I suppose this was my *sacrifice he* chose for me. I've worked on securing the Algieri account for some time now, but then he strips it all away from me with no explanation! I'm so done with his mazes and mysteries!

"I've done everything that has been asked of me. I've brought huge cases and clients to the firm. That's by far more than anyone on my floor. I deserve a little bit more respect I would think. A little more respect than him stripping away my chances at becoming partner. He acts like I'm some damn rookie advisor. How could he just auction me off like that?!

"I deserve more of him being a father who cares and less of a boss that could care less! I truly believe he gets his rocks off insulting my hard work and belittling me."

An ominous silence filled the room. Denise turned away from her flowers and faced Franklin again. She rested her hands on the island before speaking.

Leaning in, she asked, "So what are you willing to sacrifice? Your love for your father or some account that may or may not bring you the perks you're seeking?"

Franklin exhaled noisily through his pursed lips.

Chapter IX

Take only what you need, not what you want.

The more you get, then the more you have to lose.

MRS. DENISE MITCHELL, ONCE A HIGHLY touted anesthesiologist, hadn't ever been one to mince words. Especially, when it came to her speaking hard truths. She's extremely intellectual. A jet black, wolf grey haired, fiery, audacious individual just wouldn't give her full justice. She was the deeply caring mother of Franklin and loving wife to Arthur Mitchell. She recognized the frustration clouding Franklin's features. He proceeded to vent without answering her question.

"I'm okay with our relationship being what it is," he said. "We don't have to talk, Mom. Just because my alma mater isn't U of C does that mean I should be the black sheep? He doesn't have to believe I'm not a failure. We don't have to spend time or see each other every day. I just wanted to c—"

"FRANK!" Denise boomed. "Enough! Enough. How long will it be before you and your father get *PAST THE PAST,* huh?

"When will it be enough? What are *you* willing to sacrifice, Franklin? Tell your mother. Truthfully, what more is it that you want? You have a beautiful family, an all-American star athlete in your wife, a star pupil and athlete in Danielle, a great career, ability to live the lifestyle you want, nice home...What else is out there you want, son? Tell me please."

Franklin's face contorted, "Mom what do you mean? I want as much as I can have on this earth. I want a successful business! I want a father who doesn't look down on me! You don't under—"

"I do understand," she said glancing heavenward. "Lord knows I do. I understand that I've watched you for years now, and all I ever hear you do is place blame and excuse yourself from any culpability. I'm not choosing sides, but when you look at that man in the mirror what role has he played? I asked you what else is it you want and nowhere in your response was your family's peace of mind or security. Nor did I hear you ask for a better relationship with your father.

"When you were young, I tried to instill God deep within you because of times like this. I wanted you to have a deeper spiritual understanding. Everything has its own season and reason for happening. Nothing is happenstance, Franklin.

"I know you know this because I made sure to teach you this! Have you ever wondered why these things were happening in your life? Have you ever thought that maybe your father has needed you or truly trusts you more than you think? I pray each day that peace finds you two, and Lord knows y—."

"Mom?" Franklin interrupted. "All that religion and spiritual stuff is for children. I'm a long way from being a child anymore. We don't have to go through this again and again. I'm in charge of my destiny and my own fate.

"No, omnipresent being is watching every move I make. Nor is it deciding if things are good or bad. For years you've talked as if you've seen something or know for a fact this spiritual world you speak of even exists. If all that were even remotely true then where was the help today? Where was anybody to help me today?

"I can't be fully in charge of my life if I have someone, my own flesh and blood might I add, opposing me every chance he gets. I'm here in a position to win because I put myself in this position to win. No, one else! Not dad and certainly nothing spiritual, and as far as dad having some ulterior motive for us…save it."

Denise rested her hand on her cheek. Choosing her next words took care. It took resolve as she winced at the sight of her son's scowling face. Her foot tapped the tile of the kitchen floor as she finally responded, "Are you done?"

Franklin started, "I'm n—"

"It doesn't matter if you are or not. I'm telling you that you are. I have three points to make on this topic, and you can choose to do what you want with what I'm about to say.

"You're my only child and I'm proud of you, but who do you think you are to disrespect me or your father? You have worked your way up and accomplished a lot of things, but never forget where you began. There are several things you've done that I could never do, but don't you ever disrespect God or me in my house again. Understand?!"

"Yeah," Franklin scoffed.

"Secondly, no matter how overwhelming, impatient, curt, demanding, or sometimes apathetic your father may come off, he's still your father. He was there. He's always been here Frank. Making sure you had what you needed and grew up in a stable home. He's sacrificed plenty for you and for me well before you were ever a thought.

I know plenty of young men that never even knew their father. I remember it wasn't always this way. The house, the cars, and the income was nowhere at all close to the way it was back then. However, I will concede and say that it doesn't give him any justification to treat you unfairly.

"No, he isn't a saint and yes, sometimes he carries enough stubbornness for the three us. Nevertheless, baby underneath all the good and bad, suits and ties, he is only human.

"Just like you and I he has to answer for all he's done. Never forget that. Sure, he needs to get over the whole U of C thing, but let's not pretend that you didn't promise him you would go. His father went, and it meant a lot to him Frank. I think because you two are so prideful and so much alike neither of you will concede.

"Arthur has had to make some difficult decisions

over the course of his lifetime. He's also made some very foolish and deeply regrettable decisions too. Some awfully bad, but certainly not all.

"I can attest to that. I needed your father at times more than he understood, but because I knew what he was trying to do I didn't make things harder for him. What he was trying to do was cook cornbread with no corn meal, son! He understands now that his absence was hard, and now I think he doesn't want you making the same mistakes he did. He has treated me unkind in the past, but we must forgive and move on.

"No one is above forgiveness, Frank. Everyone should know in the end that what they did was worth it to keep building. It's tough on both sides. The late nights, the missed birthdays, but in the end making sure it's all worth it. The sacrifice even, but it can't be for yourself. It must be for something bigger than yourself. That's when it's real.

"I believe that's what he meant when he asked. At least that is my interpretation. What he wanted to know was if you, his son, were willing to forfeit your own self-interests for the sake of something bigger. Something greater.

"If faced with tough choices, could you make the tough decisions? I know you're upset about the account, but I'm almost certain he made the decision with your best interest at heart."

Franklin's lack of eye contact said more than his words probably could. He wasn't a tad bit concerned or willing to agree.

"Mother, I get all of that, and I would never intentionally disrespect you," Franklin said grabbing his keys from the countertop to leave. "That ship has sailed though. I'm not the same little kid running around waiting on his dad to be there when it matters most.

"I'm not that naïve little boy with concerns of trying to prove himself. I'm over it. I just came to tell you I am done with wondering what's going on in his head and that's final. I want to achieve more now because I aspire for more right now!"

"Okay, Frankie. I don't want to argue or fuss anymore about it," Mrs. Mitchell asserted. "Eventually you'll come to find out it's not about the accolades or the personal achievements. No, my dear it's about family. Although he's a little bit late, to Arthur's credit, I believe he realizes that truth now. Parenthood isn't easy.

"Anyway, that reminds me. Have you talked to Dani about leaving for school? We talk a lot you know. Spend time with your family, Frank. Don't spend so much energy trying to get even with everyone. Give that energy to your wife and your daughter. They both need you."

With both her hands, she clasped Franklin's face. Her eyes glistened as she bore into him.

"I love you," she said smiling. "Remember that you have always been my little light. The light that will guide the others out of the darkness, Franklin. Don't let ambition or greed consume you, son. That's a very lonely place to be a part of."

Franklin kissed his mother on the cheek then exited the kitchen. The wind had begun to make the trees prance as he reached the outside walkway of the home. Once back in the sedan Franklin's eyes studied the front of the brick house. He made an effort just then to absorb what he had heard from his mother.

Suddenly, his phone pinged. It alerted him of a text

message he'd received a while ago. His nose crinkled when he glimpsed down at his cell phone. It was a message from Junior. Annoyed with the mere sight of his name, Franklin became rattled all over again. The message read:

Frank, I just wanted to give you the heads up. I know how much the Algieri account meant to you, but I assure you that Mr. Algieri is in great hands now. I'll need you on Wed. at 5 pm to meet and introduce me and my team. Afterward you won't be needed to stay. Thanks bro!

Inserting his keys in the ignition, the motor of the sedan thundered as it turned over. Stomping on the gas pedal, Franklin quickly pulled away down his parent's driveway.

CHAPTER X

A change may be just around the corner.

IT WAS ONLY THREE THIRTY IN THE MORNING but Franklin was wide awake in bed. Worry had carried him far beyond the confines of his bedroom. He kept replaying Monday's events at the office over and over in his mind. There was an internal void deep within him that he couldn't fill with simple vices. The conversation he'd had with his mother and the entire office incident plagued him. It was Wednesday finally and he wasn't excited or looking forward to the transitional meeting with Mr. Algieri. The meeting was scheduled for later.

Then—cutting through the soft whistle of the air through the vents was a voice absent of antipathy or any judgment.

"Frank, what's wrong?" the voice asked.

Vivienne peered over at him from the other side of their California king bed.

"Bad dream babe?" she asked softly

Franklin's expression closed up.

"No, babe," he said. "I'm fine. Just thinking."

"About?" she asked.

"I'm leaving the firm," Franklin continued. "I'm done. After this meeting later, I don't want anything to do with Arthur. It isn't like I had anything to do with him anyway."

Confusion made Vivienne's face contort.

"What do you mean leave the firm?" she asked sternly. "Franklin you are a staple there. Are you going to throw away all your hard work from all these years? Let Junior and his cronies win?"

Still gazing at the ceiling, Franklin spoke up, "It's not about that Vivienne. It isn't about winning or losing. It's not even about Junior. He isn't as important as he wants to pretend."

"So, then what is it?" Vivienne questioned. "Are you sure it's not about winning or losing? It sure seems that way to me. It certainly would be to everyone else if you were to walk away. Babe, I know you are very disappointed in your dad, but have you reached out to him? Have you once in the last few years made a conscious effort to make things, right? I can answer that for you. No! You haven't."

"Vivienne, out of all the people who I need for support, you sure aren't being supportive," Franklin scoffed.

"Look at me," Vivienne ordered.

She turned Franklin's head to face hers.

"You know I'm here for you no matter what decision you make. But I'm also here to lend logic and reason. I love you and I know it is tough feeling the way you are feeling.

"Just don't give up on all the effort you have put in. If you simply just want to take what you have and your clients to build the fund you've always wanted then I can understand. I support that. However, is it worth starting over at this stage?

"Is it worth building a fund rather than taking the family crest of '*Mitchell & Leonard'* way into the future? Arthur can't lead it forever Franklin. Are you going to let the Maxwells solidify their stake in your father's company? Are you going to let them solidify their stronghold? Think about it. You're the last block to fall."

A muscle in Franklin's jaw twitched. Although it took much effort, he plastered a smile on his face. His eyes gleamed back at hers.

"How is it you have more confidence in the situation than I seem to have in it at times?" he asked.

Vivienne's mouth curved up into a smile before she replied, "Because I married a king, a Caesar, a conqueror of all he fancies."

She drew close and kissed her husband.

"Is that right?" Franklin asked.

"That's more than right," Vivienne confirmed.

She kissed Franklin passionately again.

"By the way, please don't forget Danielle's last game is tonight. She told me she wanted to ride with me there and ride back home with you afterward. She said something about speaking with us both about a few things but separately.

"I know you said you couldn't go, but Frank don't miss this. It means a lot to her, and it means a lot to me. Okay?"

"*Mrs. Mitchell,* I will be there," Franklin beamed. "I promise. That's sometime later this evening though. What I'm more focused on right now is a five-six, caramel queen; a shapely Georgia peach to do anything and everything with that I fancy."

"*Is that right*?" she cooed.

"That's more than right," Franklin affirmed.

He proceeded to pull Vivienne's lithe body on top of his as they began to make love into the morning hours.

CHAPTER XI

The quieter you become, the more you can hear.

IT HAD BEEN ABOUT TWELVE HOURS SINCE Franklin spoke to Vivienne. Franklin had promised his wife that he would be at Dani's game, but now he had begun calculating just how he would make it there in time. Strategically, going through city traffic at that time of day would be a challenge. The game had a start time of six, but Franklin's watch displayed the time as being *five forty-five p.m.* He was no way closer to leaving the office than the furniture inside the building. Franklin and Ms. Vega had been working diligently all day to assure the meeting went as smooth as could be. However, Mr. Algieri and his team were caught in traffic too. They also were running long behind schedule. Along with two of his assistants, Junior sat in the executive conference room across from Franklin. The room was dead silent.

Franklin glanced up at the grandfather clock located in the corner of the office. He noticed it was six p.m. on the dot. His watch was correct. Suddenly, Lisa entered the conference room. She handed Franklin a note before taking her seat beside him. It read:

'Spoke with Mrs. Mitchell just now. She asked me, 'Where are you? Why haven't you answered the phone, or responded to her texts?' She said, 'The game has started. Get there!'

Franklin's anxiety increased beyond the point he was used to after reading the note.

Lisa leaned in close to him and spoke in a lowered tone, "Mr. Algieri, is here with his CPA, lawyers, business partner, and his assistant. It's the usual group. He's in your father's office with Mr. Maxwell too."

Franklin's face twisted and reddened.

"Why are they in my father's office?" he whispered.

"I'm not sure, but it's been fifteen min— "

"*Frankie, what's wrong brother*?" Junior asked.

A sly smirk appeared on his face as he continued, "Are you okay over there, buddy? You look a little flustered. Let me say, being here is being the ultimate team player and is something to be admired. Cheer up!! Oh, and Lisa don't forget that offer still stands! The ball is in your court, dear."

Junior's face lit up with amusement as he glanced

at both of his assistants.

"Isn't that right, guys?!!" he cheered.

Franklin's expression hardened as he bore into Junior and then Lisa.

Before he could reply to the character that Junior was—a raucous laughter interrupted them. It was Mr. Maxwell. All of the men and women scheduled for the meeting also emerged. Everyone in the conference room stood up to greet all the executives and associates.

Mrs. Francine Packard was Mr. Algieri's CPA. Mr. Hollis Laurel and Mrs. Kimberly Patrick were Mr. Algieri's lawyers. Last to appear was Mr. Vincent Patricia, his business partner and Ms. Olivia Browning, his assistant.

"Well, good evening, ladies and gentlemen," Junior spoke up. "It is so nice to see everyone. Please be seated. We are very excited to kick things off now that we are all here. Help yourself to any refreshments on the back wall, and then we can get started. Mr. Mitchell will begin for us this evening. Though, he will not be staying since he has other pressing engagements to attend to. Thank you."

"Well, before he does, I would like to say something if I may," Mr. Algieri announced. "From everyone here at IPSOS we appreciate your patience and hard work Franklin. It has been more than gratifying to work with you. If the ideas that Junior has coincides with my team then guess what?"

Franklin stared Mr. Algieri into the eyes.

"What's that, Mr. Algieri?" he asked.

"Well, you can still take me out to dinner from time

to time!" Mr. Algieri shouted.

Mr. Algieri's old wizened face and thick groomed moustache stretched wide as he chuckled loudly.

"I'm only kidding, Franklin," he cautioned. "Good job! Real good job! C'mon guys! Give it up for, Franklin."

The office space filled with a mediocre round of applause.

"Okay, let's begin," Mr. Algieri charged.

Franklin forced a smile on his face. He walked to the front of the room to open the meeting. He glanced at his watch: *six forty-five p.m.* When he finished his introduction, it was seven p.m. He thanked the IPSOS team, his father, and the Maxwells as he clamored to the end of the meeting opening. He also wished everyone the best of luck and progress.

"I want to say it's been an honor and a privilege," Franklin said sincerely. "I know you all will continue to make an abundance of noise in the I.T. community space. Thank you."

Another small applause scattered the room as Franklin took his exit. Lisa followed him out into the hallway. Outside the room, Franklin was close to gagging. He leaned onto the corridor wall for support.

"Mr. Mitchell, are you okay?" Lisa asked.

"Did you catch that B.S. joke he made?" Franklin asked Lisa. "That was a total shank."

"Mr. Mitchell, I've seen your sacrifice," Lisa replied. "You've been here, and put in the best effort you could. There have been times when you put this firm way above everything else. Don't let it get to you."

All of what was said made sense. It was just another eye opener for him. He glanced at his watch again: *seven thirty p.m.*

"Damn!! I have to go," Franklin panicked. "Dani's game! Lisa, I'll see you tomorrow."

Franklin turned and pressed the elevator button, but his face filled with curiosity.

"Hey, what was Junior referring to when he said something about an offer?"

The color drained from Lisa's face.

"Nothing.... He made a co—"

Suddenly, Arthur emerged from within the conference room behind them. Franklin quickly tapped the elevator button again. He hit it repeatedly once he saw his father.

The metal box finally arrived to the floor.

"No, worries, Lisa," Franklin assured. "We'll discuss it later. Be safe. I'll see you in the morning."

"Son, hold the elevator please!" Arthur said. "I'm leaving as well. Maybe we can talk shop on the way down."

CHAPTER XII

Success or failure is only determined by where you stop.

A STRONG VEIN BECAME VISIBLE WITHIN Franklin's neck. He didn't want to see his father let alone be on an elevator with him. The elevator chimed as its doors opened up to the floor. Housed with mirrored walls and a mirrored ceiling, it appeared to be more of a mirror maze than an actual lift. Drawing her lip between her teeth, Lisa entered another elevator destined for the eighteenth floor. As she entered it, she could faintly hear Franklin beginning to shout at his father.

"YOU'RE A REAL PIECE OF WORK, YOU KNOW!" Franklin shouted. "YOU DO KNOW THAT DON'T YOU?! First, you take the account from me. Then you don't tell me why. Okay, fine, but then you have the audacity to come into *my* meeting. Why the show? Why parade around like nothing has happened? Seriously, what the hell is wrong with you, huh?

"I talked with mom and Vivienne, and for a moment they both had me thinking I should talk to you. You know, just to try and give our relationship a chance but for what? Give me one damn reason why I should even entertain the thought anymore! YOU'RE SO SELFISH MAN!"

"Son?" Arthur muttered. "I can understand you're upset, but you must trust me. I only made the decision based on circumstances I cannot explain at the moment.

"There are things you haven't been privy to that I am willing to share that I couldn't before. I have not been the best father to you, and so I understand all of the angst. Son, you must understand there are plenty of things that have happened recently. Many things have placed me in many positions to take drastic actions.

"There are things you have not been exposed to yet. You can't even imagine some of the decisions I've had to make just to be standing before you now.

"I wish I could've made better choices with you son, but we can only move ahead. Of course, I had my own goals and my own ambitions, and I realize that all of this is not what it's about son. It's about much bigger things than one's own self-gratification.

"The Lord has purpose for us all, and He doesn't make mistakes either Franklin. I see that now. I ask myself what or where I would be in our relationship if I hadn't been so obsessed. I was obsessed with creating what you're now a part of. But in the end this firm doesn't matter nearly as much as having a family."

The elevator arrived at the ground floor. Franklin with a tightened jaw and creased forehead exited at a fast pace. Arthur could barely keep tempo as he had begun to cough viciously. The noise it made seemed to rip through his thorax cavity. It stopped Franklin in his tracks.

"Pop?" Franklin called out. "Hey, man! Are you, okay?!"

Grabbing his handkerchief to cover his mouth, Arthur signaled Franklin to go on ahead.

Franklin's expression hardened again. Care nor concern were present.

"Hey, I have to go," he groaned.

Arthur started again slowly after clearing his throat, "Okay, don't trouble yourself. Before you leave, I have to say this to you though. A long time ago I was just a man with wishes to have so much more for his family than just a one room studio apartment. I wanted to attain so much of what the world could offer me. But having this role wasn't worth the countless years I've lost with you and your mother.

"It wasn't worth the sacrifices I chose to make. Some are reprehensible, and I understand that now. I sacrificed the wrong things and rid myself of people that never should have been treated the way they were.

"I was a young kid that didn't give a damn, and didn't care about anything else but having success. I WAS A FOOL ONCE! The Algieri account was huge for you I know that, Franklin. I had to do to it though!

"I'm not asking for your forgiveness because I know I may not deserve it. After so many broken promises and mistakes, Franklin you still have to believe me when I say I've always wanted the best for you."

"Pop, it doesn't really matter at this point, does it?" Franklin asked rhetorically. "It's all done and over with. You made mistakes and now you're displaying contrition? What is it? Are you checking out soon or something?

"Just save it. It's whatever now. I don't give a damn anymore. You save yourself the trouble, and don't worry about it. I'm fine. That little kid is gone now. Find him and apologize to him. Now if you'll excuse me, I have to go!"

Leaving Arthur standing in the lobby, Franklin turned and raced out the front entrance of the building. Arthur's eyes welled.

"I love you too, son," he whispered.

Arthur stood in the lobby alone. He watched his son leave out into the night.

Light rain had begun to fall. Franklin climbed into his sedan a few moments later and headed north. It was almost eight p.m. It was way past the start time of the game. He glanced down at his cell phone. He had eight missed calls and four texts. Stopping at a red light, he entered the password to access the missed texts. All were from Vivienne.

4:30 p.m. – 'Baby, Danielle and I are leaving home. See you in a bit. We love you. Be careful.'

5:39 p.m. – 'Frank, where are you? The game is starting soon.'

6:30 p.m. – 'Unbelievable! You gave me your word, Frank! You promised me you would be here! Why aren't you answering?! Is the meeting not over? This Mr. Algieri exec or whoever he is can't be more important than your damn family?!'

8:20 p.m. – 'Danielle and I are headed to your mother's. When you find the time to get your head out of your ass then that's where we'll be!'

Franklin's face went blank. The more it seemed he had it all together the more it seemed everything was falling apart. He looked out the front windshield into the rain as his eyes flickered about. He was anxious to see Vivienne and Dani. He wanted to explain everything. He truly wanted to be there. As the light turned green, he sped down the street through the night thinking of ways he would fix everything.

'*When it rains it pours!*' He thought to himself.

CHAPTER XIII

One day you may never wake up again and there won't be any more time to do all the things you've always wanted.

DANI, VIVIENNE, AND DENISE WERE ALL sitting quietly in the latter's family room. Dani batted her eyes from the family photo on the mantel.

She blew out a harsh breath before breaking the silence, "I just don't get him sometimes! Will it ever not be about him?! Why does he make promises he won't keep, and then make more promises on top of those?!"

"Danielle, I'm so sorry he missed the game baby," Vivienne said. "He tries. He surely does. When he gets here just ride home with him as you planned, and express to him everything you feel. For me, I can't tell you how much our conversation enlightened and impacted me today.

"I needed to hear all of what you said. It's important that we continue to grow and communicate as you said. It's amazing how a conversation is sometimes all it takes. I never would have thought or keyed into the way you feel about our relationship.

"Like you, I want it strong and open. As your mother I want you to have a stable relationship with your father as well. He needs both of us like you need us, and I need you both."

"Dani, I agree with your mother," Denise simpered. "Don't suffocate your feelings. Be strong and confident in expressing the way you feel no matter what. Whether it's tonight, tomorrow, or the next day. Let your father know how you feel. It's important he knows, and that you express your thoughts often and always.

"Don't keep holding onto the things you feel may make you vulnerable if you were to share them. He'll never know what it means to you unless you voice it. It's funny to think that you two are so very much alike. Both of you are more similar now than you both know. You're both my little fighters too! I'll fix us all some tea."

"Oh, that would be nice," Vivienne approved.

Dani squeezed her eyes shut. She tried hard to visualize a time when her dad wasn't always as inconsiderate or lax in his efforts to be present. It was not in a ubiquitous way, but to fully grasp the importance of the moments.

Her thoughts began drifting her away. Suddenly,

she was back at her tenth birthday party. It was May 16, 2010 and she was having a huge get together with all her friends to celebrate the occasion. She remembered there were balloons of all colors, sizes, and shapes. Since it was a dress up party, all of her friends were donned in every cartoon character costume imaginable.

A huge "Timmy Turner" mascot from the cartoon show The Fairly Odd Parents was also in attendance taking photos with the children. Vivienne even had board games scattered about in various places throughout the house. She made sure to entice enough fun for all the pint-sized invitees to have a blast. Dani could still visualize the radiant sun on that day and smell the freshly mowed lawn as her daydream carried on.

She remembered the smell of the strong cheese aroma from the dozen pizzas Vivienne ordered. The smell made her eyebrows waggle she remembered. There were tropical fruit juice pouches and excitement everywhere.

However, as the party went on, there was one familiar face Dani wanted to see but couldn't locate. This face was of a person invited by default. This was the one person she knew couldn't hide amongst her diminutive counterparts. Surely enough it was Franklin's face missing from the crowd.

Dani had not seen her dad since he had left home earlier in the morning on that day. Although it was time to cut her fluffy Confetti Vanilla Layered Cake, she didn't want to do it without him. On top of the cake, it displayed huge blue words: *We love you!*

Dani's face grimaced in real time as the old imagery replayed lucidly within her mind. Remembering the moment caused tears to roll down her cheeks. She had retained the scene.

"Mommy, where's Daddy?" she asked.

"He'll be here, baby," Vivienne replied. "Now go ahead and blow out your candles."

Dani blew out the candles of the cake. She jumped at the sound of a voice she recognized calling out to her from behind.

"DANI!" the voice bellowed.

Amongst the children, there he stood. It was Franklin! He had been inside the Timmy Turner costume the entire time. Only now he had removed the head piece.

Running and leaping into his arms she shouted, "DADDY!!"

As the children cheered in unison, she remembered hugging him affectionately.

"I told you I'd be right here, Danielle," Franklin encouraged softly. "Right here."

With tears shimmering in her eyes Dani slowly opened them to see Franklin knelt down before her in present time. Her mouth downturned as she turned her gaze away from him toward her mother.

"Honey?" Franklin muttered. "Honey, let's go home."

He extended his hand out towards her.

"*Go ahead, Danielle,*" Vivienne mouthed from across the room.

Dani begrudgingly stood up from the sleek sofa, and took her father's hand.

"Frank, I'll be right behind you two," Vivienne

said.

Franklin grabbed Dani's things and Vivienne's keys to pull her car around to the front door. They all walked out of the comfortably lit room together.

"You guys get home safe in this rain," Denise entreated. "This rain is supposed to continue through the night. The LORD will open the heavens, the storehouse of his bounty, to send rain on your land in season and to bless all the work of your hands. That's Deuteronomy twenty-eight and twelve."

Franklin parked Vivienne's sedan close enough for her not to trek in the rain. Unlatching and raising her umbrella, she walked over. Dani whispered in her grandma's ear after giving her a hug and a kiss.

"Thank you, and I love you Nana," Dani said as she smiled

"You're welcome, dear," Denise whispered in response. "I love you too, and I'll see you soon. Oh, and don't worry about what college life will change. Things will and must change for growth. You just have to grow with it. You're young Dani. Live every moment, and don't trouble yourself! Everything will go as right as it can!"

Dani's eyes narrowed. "How did you know?"

"Nana, just knows child," Denise professed. "I've had sacrifices too."

"I understand, Nana," Dani assured.

She winked at her grandmother before getting into her father's car.

"Franklin, you guys could stay the night since it's raining the way it is!" Denise suggested. "It would be nice to have you all over and out of the rain. Arthur should be home in a bit."

"Mom, we're fine," Franklin shouted through the car window. "I'll call you once we make it home."

Mrs. Mitchell acknowledged her son with a simple thumbs up as the two sedans rolled away.

There wasn't a sound to be heard inside of the sedan's cabin as it pulled down the winding road. The sound of the beating rain on the windshield was all that could be heard. Who would speak first? Both Franklin and Dani were playing a mental game of chess. Suddenly, Dani received a vibration from her cell phone. It was a text from Monica:

Good game tonight girl! It feels so good we won our last game on our home floor. Anyway, how did it go with your dad? Have you heard from him yet? Let me know if you want to talk. Get at me later for sure.

Dani looked up from her phone, and out of the passenger side window at the rows of maple trees lining the road. Doubt covered her face. She wanted to ask and tell her father so many things, but what would be different this time if she did? What could she say to truly captivate the essence of what's going on in her head? Her nostrils began to flare as she searched for the right words.

With all her heart she loved and admired her father, but in ways she pitied him. Having had enough of the unsettling silence she decided to speak openly and freely. She wanted a stronger relationship with him, and in order to do that then she had to talk to him. She maintained her line of sight out of the passenger side window at the overlapping maples.

"Dad, in all honesty I feel sorry for you," she

quipped.

"Sorry?" Franklin countered. "Did you say you feel sorry for me? Can you explain that comment because that doesn't make any sense? Why would you feel sorry for me?"

He stared at the back of Dani's head.

"Dad, you can't get out of your own way," Dani scolded. "It's bad enough that you didn't show up to my game, but what's worse is that you looked me straight in the eyes and lied to me. Why? Why even lie to me that way? I even gave you an out before you did."

Dani finally peered over at Franklin, but he wasn't reciprocating her gaze. He was quite speechless. His face glowed red as he looked ahead. He began to fidget with the windshield wipers in an attempt to bypass eye contact with his daughter.

"That wasn't rhetorical," Dani gleaned. "What? No more stories of how your meeting held you up, or how you left a document at the office you needed to go back for?

"Dad, truthfully, I'm not as upset as I was, nor do I choose to be. To be truly upset would have been to say that I expected you to be there. But in my heart, I felt you wouldn't be. At first, I had a little bit of hope that you wouldn't let me down, but then I realized it was *Mr. FRANKLIN MITCHELL* I'm dealing with here. After a while, you just kind of know what to expect.

"The funny thing is Nana just told me we were more similar than we know. I can't say I agree with her though. There is no way I would miss out on as many defining moments in my child's life as you have.

"I'm nothing like you or Pawpaw for that matter.

Maybe she meant you and he are more similar than you both care to admit. I think about all the stories I would hear you tell mom about Pawpaw, and to be dreadfully honest it's you two who are no different."

Franklin trembled as he glanced at his daughter. He wanted so much to have his father's love and respect and to be a great professional in his field, but truthfully neither of those things meant as much to him as being a better father. He loved his family very much and as many times as he wasn't there it reminded him of his own childhood. Franklin peered up into the rearview mirror noticing Vivienne's bright headlights behind them. His thoughts took him back to his conversation with her from earlier.

'Who am I becoming? As much as I've tried not to operate as my father or resemble his actions…Am I?' He thought to himself.

"Dani, listen," he started. "I apologize for not being there and dropping the ball so many more times than either one of us can count. In so many ways all three of us are each other. Pawpaw, you, and I.

"As much as I don't want to admit it, I believe the same things I dislike about him now you dislike about me. For that I apologize. In a weird way that makes you and I congenial.

"I never wanted to miss birthdays or miss games, but I did. It never dawned on me that the more I fed this anger and vitriol towards him then I would see it displayed from my own daughter. I even sound like him right now. I can't say I don't deserve it. I believe the disappointment is warranted, but you're better than me.

"To feel pity for me is to sympathize with me ironically enough. I never really felt pity for Pawpaw though. In fact, I've done the exact opposite of what you've done for me. Dani I truly am sorry for missing the game, and I was on track to make it tonight but there's no excuse I care to give. I'm going to make an effort to be better. I will be better."

"Dad, I'm not saying you're this complete absent-minded father," Dani corrected. "I love you for who you are, but I'll be leaving for Oregon soon which is very far away from home. I'm only saying I need you and mom's support now more than ever. I love you, old man! I just need you to be there."

Franklin's face lit up as he glanced over at Dani. He saw the one thing in her he knew was hard to find within himself. Forgiveness. It's not like he didn't want to forgive his own father, but it was tougher than entering the eye of a needle. This resentment that fed his anger wouldn't let him separate from the pain he had felt emotionally.

However, Dani was different. She was stronger than he was in that regard and an inspiration that it wasn't always about self-interests and self-gratification. Forgiveness shouldn't be one of those things that are hard. It takes steps to having productive and progressive relationships; that's not only with someone else but with yourself as well. Most times it's much bigger than revenge and who wronged who. It's more about moving forward.

"I love you too, Dani," Franklin said.

He glanced over and placed his huge almond hand atop youthful one.

"I love you too," Dani assured.

A dimpled smile shown on Dani's face. Then—terror transformed it just as quickly. Her gaze was looking back through the front windshield.

"DAD, LOOK OUT!!" she screamed.

Franklin had no time to react or see what Dani saw impeding their path. It was a robust white-tailed deer sprinting out right in front of them in the middle of the road. The sedan smashed head on into the wild animal. The impact of the collision sent the deer and the sedan veering deep beyond the pavement. The vehicle then smashed head-on into one of the huge Maple trees lining the roadway.

CHAPTER XIV

"Isn't it scary knowing that any time could be the last time you talk to someone?"

FRANKLIN SLOWLY OPENED HIS LEFT EYE AS the rain rhythmically pattered on his body. He was dazed and unaware of what led him lying in the middle of the road.

A tumid right eye kept him from seeing anything clearly through both eyes. He made a failed attempt to locate a face that was familiar to him. He was incoherent, awakened to a succession of flashing lights, overlapping voices, and the whooshing of helicopter propellers overhead.

He was severely battered and suffered multiple injuries to his entire body. That led to him being stiff and numb. After being unconscious for some time, he couldn't comprehend what the voices surrounding him were saying. A loud ringing in both of his ears prevented that also.

"Sir, can you hear me?" EMS echoed.

Franklin's eye searched the sky.

"He has a strong pulse present," EMS continued. "Secure his c-spine Ronnie. Sir, the emergency services are here! My name is Rachel! I am with emergency services. Can you hear me? If you can hear me, tell me what's your name."

The incessant ringing in Franklin's ears muzzled any attempt of comprehension. With the poor vision in his eye, he could only make out the movement of Rachel's blurred face and mouth.

"Sir, can you hear me?!" Rachel continued.

The sound of Rachel's voice was finally able to break through. He was finally able to discern Rachel's questioning.

"Franklin," he moaned in pain. "My name is Franklin," Where's my daughter? Where's Danielle?"

"Sir, my name is Rachel. Is it okay if we help you sir?" she asked.

"Where is my daughter?!" he moaned again. "Danielle!! Dani!!"

"Sir, we need you to calm down for us," Ronnie pleaded. "We are going to transport you to the nearest hospital. Can you tell us what happened?"

“I don’t know,” Franklin murmured.

EMS grabbed and flashed a penlight in his eyes. They checked Franklin’s left pupil.

“Sir, please look at my nose for me,” Rachel said.

Shining the penlight into his eye she began her procedure.

“Sir, can you tell me what day it is?” Rachel continued.

“I don’t know,” Franklin stammered.

Rachel spoke up, “Ronnie let’s put on the c-collar and begin the transport!”

The EMS proceeded to load Franklin on a backboard and spider strapped him in at the chest and pelvis. The straps were below and above the knees. Once he was lifted up from the ground, Franklin could see what was left of the sedan on the side of the road. It was wrapped around a massive tree.

The sedan was indescribable. Having multiple air bags deployed and being heavily damaged; it was miraculous for him to be alive. Franklin could hear his mother’s voice echoing in the distance faintly.

“Is he going to be okay?” Mrs. Mitchell asked frantically. “Frank I’m right here son! I’m here with you Frank! Vivienne is with Danielle! Hold on Frankie! Fight it!”

The rain began to downpour as the EMS raised Franklin into the ambulance. Mrs. Mitchell got in right as the service vehicle’s double doors were slammed. It then began to pull away. With his head supported by the neck brace, Franklin could only peer over slightly to get a glimpse of his mother.

He raised his hand in an effort to grasp ahold of hers. Denise’s eyes flood. She extended to grip his hand as his mouth tried it's best to curve into a slight smile. Franklin then drifted out of consciousness again.

Shortly afterwards the ambulance arrived at the nearest hospital. He was suffering a ruptured spleen, several facial contusions, a concussion, and fractures to his fibula, wrist, and collarbone.

He immediately was sedated and prepped for surgery. At the same time, he was beginning his transport from the scene of the crash, Vivienne and Dani were arriving at the very same hospital via air medical services.

Dani had a pulse, but was unresponsive when EMS arrived at the scene. She had a number thirty-four injury severity score. She had a broken clavicle, lacerated spleen, and fractures to her face, ribs, tibia, and radius. According to the Glasgow Coma Scale, within a range of 3-15, she was reading at an 8.

In the waiting room, a place of old magazines and sorrow, Vivienne and Mrs. Mitchell waited eagerly for an official prognosis for Franklin and Dani. Vivienne panted and paced back and forth as she could not contain her emotions. Both her child and husband were in hurt and there was nothing she could do to help either of them.

Feeling powerless she started thinking of reasons to blame herself. *'It should've been me. What if this is the last time, I'm able to see them both alive? What if being angry with Franklin was the last memory I'll ever have with the love of my life?'* Vivienne thought.

Anger, anxiousness, and guilt clouded her mind. She dropped to her knees in agony. She became very upset and distraught.

"What have I done?" she moaned as tears ran profusely down her cheeks. "They didn't deserve this! Oh, my babies!"

"Vivienne keep your faith," Mrs. Mitchell counseled. "It's going to be okay."

"Keep my faith?" Vivienne asked. "I want to know what's going to happen to my family now Denise. It's all my fault!"

Vivienne's lower lip quivered. She had not yet risen from the floor.

"Vivienne it's nobody's fault!" Mrs. Mitchell reasoned as she lifted Vivienne from the floor. "If anyone is at fault then it surely isn't you. It's nobody's fault but his. I just thought he said we had more time!"

With tears shimmering in her own eyes, Mrs. Mitchell comments apprehended Vivienne in her emotive state almost immediately. She peered down at the hospital floor where from where she now sat.

"What do you mean '*He said we had more time*'?" Vivienne clamored.

Even over the sounds of the television sets, clacking of computer keys, gurneys sliding down long hallways, and pitter-patter of various feet, at that very moment time eased its pace. Inner thoughts could be heard aloud.

Vivienne's eyes tightened. She wiped away her tear-soaked cheeks.

"What are you talking about Denise?" Vivienne continued. "Who is it that you are referring to?"

Mrs. Mitchell avoided Vivienne's gaze. She realized at that moment she had unconsciously revealed something she shouldn't have. That something was something that had haunted her for over thirty years.

This was the very first time Mrs. Mitchell could ever be described as impetuous. She was always very careful with her words and patient. However, she held a secret neither Vivienne, Franklin, nor anyone else knew except for Arthur knew about.

“Denise did you hear me?” Vivienne asked. “I said what are you talking ab—”

The sound of the hospital doors almost ripping open interrupted Vivienne’s train of thought. It was Arthur.

“HOW ARE THEY?!” he boomed.

“ARTHUR!!” Mrs. Mitchell clamored.

She sprang from the low-end seat over to her husband. Embracing him she crumbled in his arms. His embrace was warm, and his strong arms seemed very protective as they wrapped around her. The world around them melted away as she squeezed him back. She wished the situation was not real life. She wished she could rewind the clock of life.

“Denise how are they?” Arthur asked. “What are they saying about Danielle?! Where’s our son?”

“Arthur, we don’t know anything yet,” Mrs. Mitchell said helplessly. “We don’t have any updates.”

During the Mitchell’s entire exchange, Vivienne gave them both once overs. Her thoughts were still on what Mrs. Mitchell had just said. Although, it was vague, it was also unusually random and eerie. *What did she mean?* As she thought to herself her curiosity grew.

Normally the stoic type, Denise was visibly more upset than Vivienne had ever seen. Was the ‘*he*’ in reference to Arthur? It was just such a peculiar statement for Denise to make.

There was no doubt Vivienne wanted to know what or who she was alluding to. However, her biggest concern was of Dani and Franklin. *Would they survive this freak accident? How would things change if they did not?* She thought again.

Standing in the waiting room without any updates posed a real possibility her thoughts could be realized.

"How did you not see the deer, Franklin?" Vivienne said quietly. "I hope they weren't arguing! Please Lord I hope they weren't."

"Vivienne, I'm so sorry," Arthur lamented.

"Thank you, Arthur," Vivienne said. "But I'd be much better off if I knew what was going on. We haven't heard anything yet!"

"Listen," Arthur charged. "Everything will work out for the best. We'll get through this. THEY"RE BOTH FIGHTERS!! They won't give up. They won't give in. THEY CAN'T!!"

CHAPTER XV

Keep around the ones who heard you when you never said a word.

AFTER THE BETTER PART OF FOUR HOURS had gone by, there was still no word from anyone. Then a man who looked fatigued, thirtyish, and wearing scrubs entered the waiting area. Exhausted but composed, he peered around the room to locate someone. He was one of the medical doctors the Mitchells were all eager to see. A nurse followed closely behind him. With a solemn expression upon his face, he approached Vivienne, Denise, and Arthur. His soft steps and movements were unhurried, fluidly choreographed, and purposeful.

“Mrs. Mitchell?” the doctor asked in his deep baritone voice. “Hello, I’m Doctor Timothy Hills.”

“Hello, I’m Mrs. Vivienne Mitchell,” she replied. “This is my husband and daughter-in-law. What can you tell us?”

Vivienne’s eyes widened as she fretted the doctor’s next words. Understandably drained and distressed, she braced herself for any potential medical jargon or easy English he might use. A sudden wail from on the other side of the waiting room interrupted the doctor momentarily.

“NO!!” A woman screamed.

Standing in front of the woman was another scrub wearing clinician apparently delivering news the hearer was unhappy with. That was the norm inside the confines of that place. The drab and dreary alike. Even the hospital smell of the Iodoform, the disinfectant they use that gives most hospitals their distinctive smell, was enough to drive one mad.

“Please walk with me,” the doctor said as he returned his attention to the Mitchells. “So, as of about fifteen minutes ago both Franklin and Danielle have had successful surgeries. Franklin is currently stable, but he will still need to be monitored closely for several hours. He’s in the post-surgical recovery unit. All of the effects of general anesthesia can take several hours to wear off.

“Danielle is sedated now, and I want to be very clear with what I’m about to say; we still have a long way ahead. We are unsure at this time of her recovery time. Her vitals were dramatically elevated, and due to her trauma, she had to be placed in a medically induced coma.”

Vivienne gasped.

She covered her mouth with both palms as she raged, “Oh, no!”

Her face flushed red as her entire body went numb. His words were rich with realism, but was a far cry from the sustenance she needed or wanted. The news couldn’t fill the dark hole deep within the pit of her stomach.

“Where’s my daughter?!” she pleaded. “Can I see my daughter right now, please?! This cannot be happening!”

“Mrs. Mitchell, you can see your daughter and your husband,” the doctor declared. “They are not too far from one another. The nurse can see you to either of their rooms.”

Vivienne looked heavenward as she shut her eyes. She positioned her hands for a short prayer. She then followed the nurse down the hallway. They eventually were out of sight.

Denise embraced Arthur once again. In that very moment, his arms squeezed her tighter as she breathed more slowly. Her body snuggled into him as every muscle encapsulated her. Secretly they both knew it would take more than pentobarbital or thiopental to rescue Franklin and Dani from what was up ahead.

Chapter XVI

Train your mind to be calm in every situation.

THE BRIGHT LIGHTS OF THE HALLWAY DID nothing to illuminate the darkening gloom growing within Vivienne. She followed behind the nurse closely. Affixed beside every door she walked by was a large plastic sign, navy blue with white lettering—no fancy fonts, just all-caps with labels of room numbers. She found a little comfort seeing how tidy the hospital was.

'*At least her family wouldn't be under any medical care with a staff that didn't understand the importance of cleanliness.*' She thought to herself.

Finally, they reached the hospital room, and there she

was. Through a tiny window in the door, Vivienne could see her. Her only child was all alone. The number of things attached to her was outrageous. Dani had an IV, heart monitor, and tubes crossed everywhere. It was an unreal sight to take in. Vivienne could not fully absorb what she was seeing and nearly lost it looking over her daughter.

She could barely stand still. She was taken aback by the number of tubes running through Dani's body. Dani resembled a scientific project more than a young spry seventeen-year-old. Like any parent, all Vivienne wanted was for Dani to be well again. She had to make it through.

The compression of the ventilator's rhythmic hissing rose and fell in loudness as the machine cycled. The oxygen made a whooshing sound as it added to the gas mix. The two sounds made an unusual background melody to the noisy room.

"Oh, my baby," Vivienne whispered. "Look at my little girl!"

Vivienne walked away from the room to try and compose herself. Doubt rushed over her body in a wave of chills.

'*How will this change things? How must she approach this situation being as positive and faithful as she can?*' She thought.

She was overtaken by a deep fear and skepticism. Uncertainty spun her thoughts into a whirlwind of guilt and doubtfulness. The heavily lit hallway seemed to close in all around her.

Every second that ticked away became more valuable and more appreciated. Emotionally she was spent. It was as if someone had suddenly locked away her peace of mind in some strange clandestine place.

Inside Franklin's room, both Arthur and Denise Mitchell sat in total silence. His room wasn't as gaudy as Dani's, but it was still plain inside the colored room. Franklin would be calling the drab place his home until he recovered fully. An old television was mounted on the wall near the door. In the corner were two chairs that completed the sparse décor.

A window with a view of the parking lot below was as close to the outside Franklin would have for the near future. This was truly the place his parents knew he'd be tested before leaving its dull walls. Nothing would be safe for him within a short while.

The silence inside the room was ominous. The repetitive hissing and binging of the machinery did more to break their quietness than either one of them attempted to. But still their thoughts were in the same place. Both pondered how in the world they would explain to Franklin what things lied ahead for him. What could they possibly say that would have him believe their cryptic yet factual story? Truthfully, it was still hard for them to even believe it themselves.

"Have you told him yet?" Denise asked quietly.

She looked as though she was in a trance. Her eyes were fixated on the mechanical bed where Franklin lain. She was enraptured by what had taken place. Denise knew of all the reasons why Arthur had to make an effort to announce the things she inquired about.

"Everything you do in this world you must answer for," she bemused. "Arthur?! Have you told our so—?"

"Denise?" Arthur interrupted. "No, I have not told our son his dad's dying; nor, have I told him why. But then telling him why would mean his father is the horrible person he's always believed him to be.

"Isn't that it? Am I the horrible father he believes? I've been such a fool to think everything else was more important than this. My fa—!"

"Arthur, *YOU ARE HIM!*" Denise pressed. "Do you not remember what Daniel said? You have to tell Franklin the truth."

Mrs. Mitchell's eyes began to swim with tears.

"Denise, it's been over thirty years," Arthur proclaimed. "I feel the same now as I did then, and I'm sorry for all that has been done. Yes, it's my fault, but I can fix this!"

As he stood at the end of the hospital bed, Arthur's eyes focused in on Franklin's still body. As he lain there, Arthur watched him sleep the same as when he was a child. He was as still as the waters of Lake Oconee. Arthur remembered when they would visit the beautiful body of water during the summer months so many years ago.

The pain of telling Franklin the truth was a prison for him. In that prison of fear and confusion, the agony persisted. As the hours came and went, Vivienne suggested that Denise and Arthur stay with Franklin while she stayed with Danielle. Ultimately, Vivienne wanted to be with Danielle. She was in much worse shape. She wanted to be alone with her daughter if this was to be their last moments shared together.

The hour drew further into the night as Denise Mitchell finally dozed off. She had snuggled herself beneath Arthur's jacket.

However, Arthur couldn't sleep. He felt overburdened by the weight of the words he was trying to gather. The tick of the secondhand from the room's clock began to drown out the medical machines inside the undersized room.

It was just a little before dawn when Arthur moved one of the frayed hospital chairs closer to Franklin's bedside. He had wanted to sit closer to his son. He watched as his son's chest compressed simultaneously with the ping of the heart monitor beside him. Arthur's stomach tightened.

Suddenly, Arthur began speaking to him softly, "Son I want to say I love you and your mother with all of my heart. Maybe my affection for you both is greater now than it's ever been."

He clutched ahold of Franklin's hand as he spoke. Arthur's enormous hand nearly enclosed Franklin's muscular hand entirely as he gripped it tight. Becoming choked up, a muscle in Arthur's jaw twitched. Covering his face within his hands he couldn't bring himself to finish what he had set out to do.

"I can't do this," he groaned.

Just as he had begun to give up speaking to Franklin, his wife's hands were felt upon his back and shoulders. They had begun to massage him. His weary physique screamed for comfort as the soft hands massaged deep. Denise was awake again and comforting her husband.

She caressed Arthur as he remained seated. She wanted to alleviate the settled stress and anxiety deep within his sturdy frame. Rolling and rotating her own neck around, she began feeling the effects of sleeping in a wooden hospital chair. The old chair had definitely seen brighter days.

Although she was tired from her overnight stay at the hospital, she felt more inclined to attend to her husband than to herself and sleeping preferences.

"Arthur I'm here," she said in a warm voice. "I'm right here. Take a deep breath and relax. When Frank wakes up just be honest, and don't hide from the truth he needs to hear. He's a fighter Arthur, and you're a fighter. We're a family. Therefore, we'll get through this together."

Arthur reached to rub his hand through her hair as she leaned in closer onto his back. Her curled black and grayish locks always were capable of bringing him a joy he couldn't put into words.

Her locks hung in more waves than curls, but that didn't matter to him. Her warm body close against his body relieved his stress for the moment. Denise was a relief to his anxiety more so than any medication could ever have been. Her embrace could never be long or tight enough for him not to want it consistently. He felt her soft skin and her gentle squeeze on his own skin, and it was heaven.

In her arms he knew he was safe and his troubles were set at ease if only for a short while. In that embrace he was loved no matter how many mistakes, disappointments, or letdowns he'd made. He allowed himself to be engulfed in her warmth and her strong presence. He had begun to make peace with himself in that moment of tranquility.

"Arthur, when he wakes up don't be afraid and don't worry," Denise whispered as she grabbed her purse. "He'll understand. He'll see."

"But if he doesn't?" Arthur broke in.

"If he doesn't then Daniel will show him," Denise responded. "He won't have a choice to not see then. Anyway, my dear I'm going to run home and take a shower. I can bring you some fresh clothes."

"No, honey I'm fine," Arthur confirmed. "I got everything right here. This connection with him is what I should've wanted in the first place. No amount of money in the world can compare to what I missed with our son. Don't worry though, Denise. I love you, and I always will. Go on home. I'll tell him everything."

Arthur winked his eye as he glanced over at his exhausted wife. It was his way of saying that things would be fine. The corners of Mrs. Mitchell's mouth lifted.

"Okay, love," she said. "I love you too, and I'll see you in a bit."

Turning back around in his chair, Arthur noticed Franklin was awake and staring right at him. His face was still bruised and swollen, but his left eye didn't blink at all. He opened his mouth to speak for the first time. He was as motionless as a camouflaged animal sensing a predator.

"Tell me what?" he moaned.

The effort to say those words took a lot of strength to say.

"Where am I? Where is everyone?"

Chapter XVII

Healing is forgiving yourself

ARTHUR FORCED A SMILE ON HIS FACE. He knew what he had to say would put all their trust and everything Franklin knew about his family into question. If Arthur could rewind time to hold Franklin's newborn frame close to his or to see him smile when he made his first jump shot—it was then. Franklin was still feeling the effects of his injuries. He grunted and grimaced from every slight movement made. He was trying his best to position himself more comfortably atop the bed on wheels.

"Son, I have something to tell you because it's time for you to know the truth," Arthur asserted. "One day I was told that this day would come, but I pretended for so long that it never would. Unfortunately, I was too foolish then to realize what effects my pride and selfish ambitions would have on the people I love the most."

"Answer my question first, Pop," Franklin mumbled. "Where's everyone? Where is Dani?"

A silence filled the hospital room as Arthur gathered his thoughts.

"Franklin, don't get worked up," Arthur said. "You need your strength. "Danielle is in a coma right now. You both were hurt, but her injuries were far worse than yours."

Franklin's face contorted as his left eye blinked rapidly.

"No!" Franklin raged. "Not Dani!"

He attempted desperately to rise out of bed.

"I have to see her!" he remarked. "Where's Viv?"

Franklin screamed for Danielle as he choked himself up viciously in doing so.

"Son, please," Arthur demanded. "Stop, please? Vivienne is with Danielle now. There is no reason you should be attempting to leave your bed Franklin! You are in no condition to do that. Do you want to do more damage to your body than has already been done? Stop being a jerk for one minute and listen to me, please? I have to tell you something before I am unable to."

Arthur's thoughts flashed back to their argument the

day before. He gazed deep over his son's injured body. All the emotion and fear of what he had to do resonated deeper now.

It was if he were swimming in a vast ocean of the dark unknown without any knowledge of what dangers surrounded him or what was underneath him.

Franklin's efforts to get out of the hospital bed were halted by what his father said. Squinting his eye, he took in the sight of his father's timeworn face.

"What do you want?" Franklin huffed. "What is it that can't wait to s—?"

"You were not our first child, Franklin!" Arthur quipped.

His brow furrowed from the intensity of his inflection. Franklin's face froze colder than a block of ice by his father's comment. Arthur paced and stared up at the ceiling. Though his temperament was at a resolve he believed he could manage. Several emotions had begun to build up within himself.

In a monotone voice he sat back down and continued, "You had an older sister Franklin. Her name was Danielle.

"You and *my mom* had a daughter before me?" Franklin inquired. "You're kidding me, right? I don't understand why would you tell me this now? Why wouldn't Mom have told me? Where is she at?"

Arthur's forehead strained with wrinkles as he leaned back deeper onto the wooden chair. As he folded his arms, he looked away from his son. He directed his gaze out toward the rising sun.

"Well, where is she Pop?" Franklin asked. "Since both of you guys are keeping secrets. Where is she? You know ever since I was a kid you have always had an innate ability to speak out of your ass! I mean what is this you're telling me right now?

"So, if I had a sister then where is she?! I tell you what, Pop, gather your things, get the hell out of here and don't come back. You're a pathetic old man willing to do anything to get a rise out of me! You have the audacity to bring this up while I'm lying here and my daughter is clinging to life? I don't want to hear any more of this trash!"

"This is when I was told I had to," Arthur countered. "Franklin there are just things you don't understand."

"I don't understand?" Franklin rattled on. "No, I understand it fully. You're crazy!"

"I know your mind is probably spinning out of control right now, but your mother and I seriously had a daughter before you. Tragically she died before you were born. I killed her."

"WHAT?!" Franklin stormed. "Say that again."

"Son, I killed her," Arthur revealed. "But it is not in the way that you think. It's much more complex and complicated than that alone."

"Man, get the hell out of here!!" Franklin boomed.

Arthur's disappointment in himself had begun to elevate. He attempted to find the strength and courage he patterned his whole life around to explain himself fully. Walking toward the fifth story window, he glared out into the horizon. Reminiscing about his youth, he remembered those days as being crazy anxious times.

Building a career and starting a family at the same time wasn't an easy task. Arthur was a wiser more intelligent man now than he was back then. He had a beautiful family now, and was the head of his own successful business. But untold secrets of the family's past were now back to bare all.

"What didn't you understand about getting the hell out of here?" Franklin piped. "I mean it. I can't stand looking at you man. You're a poor excuse for a father, but an even poorer excuse of a man."

The hospital door opened up to reveal a young woman in its opening. She couldn't have come any sooner as Franklin had begun to lambast Arthur. She peered inside. It was one of the nurses arriving to check on Franklin's current status, and began his post-op care.

"Good morning, Mr. Mitchell," the nurse exclaimed. "I see you are awake early today. How are you feeling?"

"Today is not a good day," Franklin said. "Not under any circumstances."

Chapter XVIII

"Some people look for a beautiful place, others make a place beautiful." – Hazrat Khan

ARTHUR BROKE HIS GAZE FROM LOOKING at the horizon. He wanted to face his son now that the attending nurse had finally left the room. Franklin stared deep into the wall beside his bed. It was if he were trying desperately to see through it. Maybe there was some faraway place he could escape to other than where he was presently. By then he had settled down some. He had been medicated some.

Arthur continued, "Son, over thirty years ago your

mother conceived what would be our first-born child. It was a little girl, your sister. However, not even a few hours old, she had contracted a very bad lower respiratory infection. Your mother and I were told that the infection was mild, and that we shouldn't worry.

"But I remember being very worried. It was mainly because at that time I was completely broke. I had no money, and we were barely scratching by. I was a young twenty something year old with a wife and a newborn I couldn't support. We were so young Franklin. So young.

"I remember being at the hospital spent out of my wits with anxiety. I never knew it would be the place that all of our lives would change forever. So, I remember during Denise's recovery I would stay at the hospital and sometimes find myself in the lobby. So, on no special day there, I was standing at a water fountain near the waiting area. I believe it was on the second afternoon when I heard it."

"Heard what?" Franklin asked.

"I overheard this loud and very unusual laugh coming from the waiting room area," Arthur replied. "This guy was laughing just loud enough not to get a quick reaction from the staff. At first glance he seemed to be a very high-spirited guy. He was sort of a very high-strung type of guy. It was weird to say the least, but I walked over and introduced myself. I sat next to him and began a conversation.

"I asked him what could be so funny in a place like a hospital. The man gave me a wide grin and told me it was the perfect place to laugh and smile. He told me, 'He was reminiscing about a moment he'd shared with his wife some time ago.' It turns out that this stranger's name was Charlie. That same man became my listening ear over the next few days as I waited for any new updates concerning our respective families.

"He said he was there at that time due to his wife. She was very ill. In all honesty I think I was somewhat comforted by having someone to speak to.

"Charlie had told me he worked as a tour guide at some resort and did moonlight construction work. He said he was also struggling to take care of his family though. But he loved his job. I don't know why, but I never asked him what company or where he was a guide.

"He kept saying 'He'd give up anything in the world just to have one day to share with his wife again.' Later on, he had mentioned she probably wouldn't survive her illness, but he was becoming more accepting of that fact.

"Of course, Charlie's situation was different. I told him about my struggles, but that it was a different type of struggle for me being a young financial advisor during that period.

"Being a few years out of college, and not really knowing how I would support Denise and Danielle was eating away at me. Then that was when he finally looked at me and asked a question I'll never forget.

"It was though everything around us became muted. The clacking of keys behind the receptionist's desk over and over again; all of it just stopped. Charlie's demeanor dramatically changed as he spoke up.

"What does sacrifice mean to you?" he asked.

"He was staring into my eyes with an intensity I'll never forget. He continued by saying 'You have two options to choose from. Which would you choose? A successful career now and enough money to support a family later in life, or a successful career later with a healthy little girl and wife now?"

"As a joke my mouth responded quicker than my mind processed the question he'd asked," Arthur said. "Maybe it was the desire of my heart that had processed it. My exact words were, 'Are you kidding? I choose having a successful career!' I remember it like it was yesterday.

"I must've laughed too hard at the question or answered incorrectly because he just stared at me. He stared at me with his bright green eyes until the awkwardness forced me to look away. Suddenly, it felt like everything was louder and reverberating stronger again. I remember the clacking of the receptionist's keys and the rattling wheels of stretchers on the plain grey floors returning. Things felt eerily weird.

"Charlie stood up. He reached out his hand to shake mine. His trimmed nails and leathery soft skin surprised me. They didn't feel like the hands of any construction worker I knew. He said to me, 'I guess that settles it huh, friend? I'll be seeing you around Arthur. Same time tomorrow?' Then he left out of the waiting room, and I never saw him in the hospital again.

"The very same night, Danielle's infection flared up again. It had taken a dramatic hold on her frail body, and the next day she was gone, son. It was unexplainable! I mean she succumbed to the second bout of the infection almost immediately.

"All of the medical staff assisting Denise said it was one of those rare cases. They couldn't tell us more than that. Traumatized was not even the word I would use. I don't know why, but I thought back to what Charlie had asked me the day before.

"Once Denise was finally released from the hospital, I was called by an old professor who introduced me to Leonard. He mentioned he was seeking someone with a high degree of intelligence, passion, and ambition to create and get the job done in his field of work.

"All of it was just very odd that one day I had no professional prospects with a sickly newborn then dramatically out of nowhere a great potential prospect with a child no more.

"At the burial a few days later, I recognized someone at the cemetery in the distance. Have you ever looked into a crowd and seen someone that just doesn't belong? It was him! It was Charlie! There was no doubt in my mind that it was him! When I saw him that time, he was well-dressed. He had on a tailored black suit with a matching black tie. His chiseled jaw was lifted in an exalted way. He stood like a foreign dignitary staring directly into my direction. I looked away for a split second, and he was gone again."

"Pop, you're not making any sense," Franklin whispered. "You are all over the place. What does this guy have to do with my parents hiding the fact that I had an older sibling? Neither one of you thought it was necessary to tell me this after thirty years?

"Why is this guy even important right now? First, I had a sister but now you're implying something mysterious happened to her. It sounds like she died in a way that had nothing to do with Arthur Mitchell's vanity."

"Son," Arthur started again. "Just hear me out. Do you remember the man you saw when you went over to our house the other day? Your mother told you his name was Daniel. Remember?"

"I remember the guy," Franklin replied. "So, what?

Don't distract me from the fact that you two hid this from me! Forget about Daniel, Charlie, and whoever else! Neither of you told me. Can't you just go away!"

"Frank, you saw that man the other day because he wanted you to see him," Arthur continued. "He has unfinished business with me and new business with you. That man's name is not Daniel, and he is also not in the Estate Planning business either.

"He has gone by many names. I knew him as Charles Gideon, and he was the same man from the hospital over thirty years ago."

"Wait a minute!" Franklin resumed. "Wasn't Charles Gideon your old friend from twenty years ago? That's Mr. Charlie?!"

"It's very difficult and bizarre I know, but it is the truth," Arthur warned.

"So, you're telling me now that the guy I saw the other day is Mr. Charlie?" Franklin teased. "The guy from the other day was a young guy. So, now Mr. Charlie is thirty years younger, and calling himself Daniel?"

The corner of Franklin's mouth quirked up. He slowly shook his head in disbelief.

"Old man you're hysterical," he continued. "This cuts the cake on low. I cannot believe what you're doing. Pop, I'm asking you to leave now. Can't you just leave me alone?! Go away! I don't want to hear any—"

"In the end it isn't dying that scares me, but the pain of knowing when," Arthur interrupted. "If a person doesn't wake up in the morning, they will know nothing of it. However, Franklin, I always want you to remember it isn't ever about what you gain in this world. It is only about what you are willing to sacrifice and endure to change the lives within it. I love you. My only regret is that I didn't say it more often. You know now though. If you want me to leave then I will leave. Goodbye, my son."

Arthur gathered his things and began to make his exit. Just then on the outside of the hospital door there were three knocks. Arthur and Franklin both glanced at the door. The wide metal enforced door crept open slowly. It was the nurse returning to check in on Franklin.

"I guess I'll be going," Arthur announced again.

He caught his son's eyes once more before walking out. Impressions of dried tears could be seen on Franklin's cheek. Arthur was a man with memories that both warmed and haunted him. He knew of the choices Franklin would soon have to make, and he couldn't shield him from it. This was the end, but still only the beginning. Stranger things lied ahead.

Chapter XIX

Eyes are useless when the mind is blind.

"WELL, WELL, WELL, FRANKIE, I THINK you're doing all you can and then some to escape hard work these days," a voice said.

Several days had gone by since Arthur had come to visit, but no one else since. Opening his eyes from resting, Franklin's surprise turned into disgust quickly. Standing at the foot of his bed was Junior Maxwell.

"So, Franklin, I see you traded a magnificent boardroom for a stodgy little hospital one," Junior said as he chuckled. "Please tell me that I'm not that intimidating that you had to do this to yourself up this way to stay away?"

"What do you want, Junior?" Franklin asked weakly. "That's convenient. So, you show your face here now? Where's your dad? You're never too far from being up his ass."

"See that's what I admire about you, Frank," Junior started again. "You always commence to smiling even when you've lost. I wanted you to know personally that the IPSOS deal is done, and I'll be a partner in your father's firm soon enough. Plus, I'm going to make for damn sure no Mitchell is mentioned above Maxwell.

"I'm going to make your life a living hell, Frankie baby, but then again that's if we decide you're worth the effort of keeping around."

"Junior, there is something I'd like to tell you," Franklin mumbled. "Before you leave you have to know this. That is if you ever wanted to know how I really feel about you."

"Sure," Junior replied. "It's not like I need anything more to laugh at, but go ahead!"

"Great," Franklin mustered. "On everything I hold dear, you are the absolute biggest heap of trash your mother could have ever pushed out of her!"

Junior's face turned crimson red. The tension between the two men was more than just a professional rivalry. Junior's malcontent for Franklin and his father stemmed from the acquisition of his grandfather's declining firm. Several years ago, the Mitchells and the Leonards took over the Maxwells firm in a buyout.

It was something that ate away at the Maxwells.

Every day they saw their grandfather's firm being taken away piece by piece by Arthur. Junior's internal pain of it all made him feel much like the Greek Titan Prometheus. He alone was Franklin's biggest rival and threat in the hierarchy of the firm. He was an Ivy League graduate and former athlete who thrived in competition. His obsession to not only win but crush his opponents, fueled him. Underneath, he reveled in other's discomfort.

"Franklin, you should take the act on the road. Through it all you're still just damaged goods hiding behind your father. You're not even next in line to take over the firm! That would be my father!

"For all of the reasons I hate you and your old man, at least Arthur walked his own path. What a pity you've walked in his shadow your whole life! You would think you'd be tired of fetching the old man's slippers! Either way, you're done whether you croak or not! At least if you leave you save yourself the embarrassment."

Franklin lunged at Junior in an unsuccessful attempt to grab him. In the attempt he agitated his wounds. He cried out in pain. Unable to reposition himself, he asked Junior for help. Franklin was hanging halfway out of the bed slumped over.

He winced in pain as he asked for help, "Junior, can you plea—"

"What was that, Mr. Mitchell?!" Junior asked sarcastically. "Say that again! I believe I heard you almost ask me for help. Can you repeat that for me?! I didn't hear you!"

"Junior, help me," Franklin clamored weakly. "PLEASE!"

"Address me as sir when you're speaking to me,

Frank," Junior proceeded. "Tell me you were never better than me. Maybe then I could help you."

Franklin pleaded, "Plea—"

"You see Frankie my hands are full anyway," Junior snorted. "I have *you* by the balls in one hand, and your daddy's firm in the other. So, sorry old buddy. I can't help you. I don't have the time these days.

"Besides I have to go see the wife. Oops, I mean your wife. I'm sure she'll love the box of candy I got for her. By the way, I don't know if you know it or not, but your father's dead."

Franklin had begun to breathe very rapidly. The numbers on the medical machines surrounding him started to crescendo.

"I just thought I'd mention that to you. So sad. The old bastard croaked in his office. Oh, well. I'm sure your mother wouldn't mind me telling you."

Junior, walked back toward the door and exited the room. He left Franklin slumped halfway out of bed. The middle-aged man was neither empathetic nor at all bothered by Franklin's state. The man's own self-interest and cockiness superseded everything else.

Along with his father, their plan was in full swing. Junior would become partner now. A coup would no longer be necessary for the Mitchells to be ousted. With Arthur gone and Franklin near it, again the Maxwells could regain control of their family's firm. They would be in sole possession of all the many assets under management.

Hanging from the bed, Franklin attempted to regain his position once more. It didn't work. The nurse arrived to his room and rushed over to aid Franklin. Pulling the man up and back into bed was not an easy task, but she finally did so. Franklin's face shown weariness and fright as his monitor's numbers continued to dance.

Junior's behavior had given Franklin a sudden panic. His blood pressure increased rapidly, and his breathing had become harsh. He stared upward into the luminescent light above him.

"Mr. Mitchell, can you hear me?!!" the nurse asked. "Mr. Mitchell?!"

The nurse ran to the hospital door and screeched out as she sought assistance. Suddenly, out from behind a corner came the attending doctor and other hospital personnel with a crash cart. The rattle of the wheels seemed to add more damage to the stripped hallway floor than anything else.

Once back into the room, the nurse laced her hands with gloves. The doctor checked Franklin's vitals. The respiratory and pharmacy teams also arrived in the room to manage Franklin's breathing.

Franklin had not ceased his gaze at the light high above him as his eyes were wide open now. He sweated profusely. It drenched his face as the doctor checked his pupils for dilation. Another ICU nurse began recording all the actions of the team. An anesthesiologist arrived thereafter. The room appeared to be a melee of bodies.

"I need a blood workup stat!" the doctor ordered. "This may be hypovolemic shock. Maintain his pulse! What's his rhythm check?"

As the doctor continued directing the traffic in the room, the once luminescent light high above them all faded quickly out of Franklin's focus.

Chapter XX

A beautiful face will age. A perfect body will change,

but a beautiful soul will always remain.

"SON, IF YOU CAN HEAR ME I WANT YOU to know your mother loves you," Mrs. Mitchell professed. She tried desperately to hold back her tears. "I'm here with you dear. It's just you and I.

"Ms. Vega visited a short while ago, and Vivienne is down in the chapel. I don't know how long she can keep it together. Although, Dani is still in a coma, I want you to know that she is in stable condition too dear."

Mrs. Mitchell sat beside Franklin's bedside clutching her son's idle hands. Her demeanor was not one of melancholia but of solidity. She was determined to see all proverbial debts paid in full and all accounts settled. Her eyes watered as she began to confirm Arthur's inevitable fate.

With a gentle calm, she continued, "It's been three days since they induced you son. How you went into shock I don't know, but you're a fighter dear. You will have to FIGHT HARD to make it back to us! I don't know what Arthur was able to tell you the other day, but Frankie I hope he told you what I have known to be true for quite some time.

"I knew that everything in your father loved you very much, and he would have done anything for his family's security and longevity. ANYTHING! But he wasn't perfect Frank. He made some mistakes he had to answer for. We all have, and we will.

"Two days ago, I want you to know your father passed on. Although I knew it would happen this way, it seems everything I have has been taken away from me now. All of a sudden everything is out of my control. I could hate him for what he did to our family, but what would that solve for us here and now? I buried your older sister, also named Danielle, years ago, and now I will have to bury your father too. BUT HEAR ME!! I WILL NOT BURY YOU NOR DANI!!

"Do you hear me, Frank?! So, when Daniel reveals himself to you, I have faith son that you will know what must be done. Let what must be done be done!"

Mrs. Mitchell glanced at her child as she rose to leave the room. Franklin was a man she knew had many demons and much sadness, disappointment, and rage within him.

Franklin was a man she watched grow from just a prayer to the intelligent, kind, and loving person he also was.

She knew he didn't ask for any of what was about to happen. However, it was time, and life didn't care what you asked for or didn't ask for; nor whether you were prepared or unprepared. It didn't matter. In life's game, unlike man's game, it does not care about sex, race, religion, creed, heritage, orientation, beliefs, opinions, or theories.

The only thing life concerns itself with is balance. Franklin like everyone else had choices, and based on what was chosen would determine what was given. Mrs. Mitchell knew it, and Arthur knew it.

"I love you, Frank," Mrs. Mitchell whispered. Then she turned and exited the room.

Chapter XXI

No one is coming to save you.

This life is 100% your responsibility.

SUDDENLY, ALL THE LIGHTS INSIDE OF THE hospital room started to shutter at a rapid pace. They were seemingly losing their voltage. The bulbs eventually popped overhead. Smoke and soft hissing sounds flowed from the panels that covered the ceiling lights. As abruptly as they had given way, the conducting wires began to illuminate all over again. This time more fiercely than before. The brightness from the wires began to intensify. The temperature inside the room began to rise almost simultaneously.

Franklin's thermal temperature increased as the room temperature level increased. His body became drenched in sweat. Forcibly, he tried to open his eyes causing him to squirm about. Finally, he awakened from his reposed state. He gasped for air. His vision was somewhat blurred but slowly coming back into focus. He was physically groggy and spent.

He called out, "Nurse!!"

Once he regained his wits, he noticed he didn't have any tubes within his body nor were there any monitors surrounding him. He wasn't even stitched or bandaged. No contusions, soreness, or broken bones either. He could also see out of both eyes. He peered around the heated room.

All at once he caught in his vision a dark cloud manifesting itself inside the center of the room. The manifestation slowly formed into the shape and body of a man. It was tall with piercing green eyes, a vigorous build, and somber expression highlighting his face. Whatever it was couldn't have been flesh and bone.

Covered and dressed in all black, it began walking slowly over to the hospital bed Franklin was still seated on. As it loomed forward with every steady step, the clapping of his newly formed all black shoes echoed throughout the incandescent room.

"NURSE!!" Franklin yelled again. "Who are you?! HEY, NURSE!!"

The figure never seemed to blink as it watched Franklin. The figure's searing oval shaped eyes could burn holes through solids on command if they wanted to. Franklin became more frightened and disheveled, but he couldn't take his eyes away. The figure was like a bad car wreck on the highway. You know you shouldn't spectate, but the sensation to look at it was too great.

"What are you?!" Franklin shrieked. "Okay, I gotta wake up! I'm dreaming, man! This isn't real that's it!"

The figure leaned in closer and spoke in a low foreboding voice. It placed its newly formed hand gently on Franklin's shoulder. The manifestation's appearance resembled an ad model at first glance, but something about its speech would cause the thought to fleet as quickly as it was conceived. It seemed as if the heat from the room was sourced from the figure itself.

"Allow me to elucidate!" it said in a grungy pitch.

The hospital room appeared to crumble all around them simultaneously. The light fixtures completely shattered as the ground quaked. The beam from the bright lights were now all but gone. A blanket of charcoal colored blackness covered the room, and like sandpaper the heat was still dry and scratchy.

To Franklin's amazement, the figure never flinched or took its gaze away from him. Its direct contact was steady, deep, and laser focused on Franklin's movements. Then the figure, now resembling the embodiment of a man's form, transposed the milieu within seconds. It revealed a horrific sequence. Without any struggle, Franklin stood up by his own power.

He called out again, "NURSE!! Can anybody hear me??!!"

He received no response. Franklin snapped his eyes shut. He'd hoped he was only dreaming the things he was seeing. But that would prove to be wishful thinking. The environment now appeared to be an empty hospital room that was no longer his.

He was able to deduce they were most likely still in the same hospital. The décor and color schemes were the same. No hardcore analyzation was necessary. The room they were in was vacant and a size larger than his original room.

Franklin, donning his hospital gown, desperately tried to make sense of what was happening. Was he dreaming? It seemed too real to be a dream, but if it were real then what happened to his injuries?

'*I have to be dreaming!*' He thought.

Was Arthur telling him the truth? His thoughts were lucid, but any hope of capturing clarity was proving to be futile. The figure, now posed as a man, never turned to look at Franklin. He was now staring intently at the door of the room.

'*What was he staring at?*' Franklin thought.

"Whatever this is I don't want any parts of it!" Franklin announced. "Wake up, Frank!! C'mon, wake up!!"

In an instant, numerous people stormed into the room. Unaware of each other's presence, the crowd of people moved about in a panic. They appeared to be a small group of hospital staff. They were all wearing scrubs as they wheeled in a young woman on a stretcher. A very loud commotion from the group ensued.

None of the people before Franklin appeared to be real. They were a part of a vision that the manifestation wanted Franklin to see. Quietly he drew closer to take a better look at what was happening. He could clearly see a young woman on a stretcher, but after getting closer he realized it was Dani.

The man had transformed Franklin's surroundings. He had Franklin viewing Dani's exact arrival into the hospital on the night of the accident.

"DANI!!" Franklin yelled. "Danielle!!"

He screamed for her, but no one could hear him. Then as quickly as the vision appeared to them it also quickly faded. The surrounding area began to lose its lighting. Nothing could be seen except for the gaze of the man in the dark.

Once again, he transposed the atmosphere. This time it changed into a darker uncontained environment. It was of some distant deserted land with nothing in sight. Dirt covered the landscape for miles in every direction. Howls and screams could be heard all around them at a booming pitch and fidelity. A pungent decay was in the air. The distinctive smell of sulfur filled the airways of Franklin's nose to such a degree it made him gag profusely.

He was no longer in his hospital room, nor was he draped in the flimsy gown they dressed him in. Due to the low visibility, he could barely see the figure standing right in front of him. A tornadic wind blew violently. The whooshing and gusting of the wind swept up small twisters of debris along a long pathway Franklin was now standing on.

He was more frightened than ever before. The dark skies filled with an unnatural overcast. Sheets of water begin to fall heavily as Franklin's feet sank down into the sediment. Buckets of water fell. He tried running away, but there was nowhere to run to. He couldn't move from where he was standing.

He tried screaming out as before, but his voice did not carry through the chaos happening all around him. He tried desperately again to move, but he was stuck in place.

"I can't move!!" he burst out. "Where am I? What is this place?!! SOMEBODY HELP ME!!!"

The mysterious figure began to walk toward Franklin from his position. As he gradually drew closer to him, the storm began to subside almost entirely by the pace of his stride. The image of a man without a flaw, and without any ego came closer. He was not wet from the heavy rains nor was he dirty from the debris polluting the strong winds. He was autonomous. He was subservient only to inevitability.

Chapter XXII

Karma doesn't spare anyone.

THE SEDIMENT UNDERNEATH FRANKLIN'S bare-naked feet began to loosen. With little to no effort he was then able to gain his footing. His surroundings were still empty and barren. Nothing could be heard except for the baying of voices and the wind howling like wolves at the moon. Franklin couldn't see anything except for the recent manifestation of a man looming closer to him. The man stood tall, and free from blemish. It gave Franklin an appraising glance.

Franklin's breathing had increased rapidly. It took him

a moment to gather himself. He finally did so long enough to ask, "WHAT IS THIS PLACE? WHO ARE YOU?!!"

Within his own rampant thoughts, Franklin finally heard the personification speak up, "You may have known of me some time ago. The man you called Charlie and the man you called Daniel you be familiar to you. But I am neither the human beings Daniel nor Charlie. I have not ever been here or there. I am Both. I am negative. I am positive. I am pain, and I am joy. Although reasons are unknown to you now, your presence here is simple. Circumstance is always decided by choice, and choice is always led by circumstance."

'*Choice?* Circumstance?' Franklin thought.

"There is only one inevitable task I have and must seek into perpetuity. It is the task of measuring. It is proportion of all things left that are out of alignment with all things right. Proper proportion if not sought will seek, but is as sure as birth triggers death. It is the order of all things alternative. Hence it is only choice that has brought you here, and it will only be by choice that decides how much equilibrium is caste out. Choice is the reason you are standing in a place where a man's soul can either be redeemed or condemned."

Franklin could not form any words to respond. He was visibly distraught and found it hard to believe what he was witnessing. He held his hands close to his eyes and face as the winds continued its drubbing onto his body.

"Choice is the gateway to any living soul's destination," Both continued. "This place is what men have called a darkened place. You are in the '*In Between*' of neither here nor there, but every step that is made will create the path which is traveled."

Franklin never broke eye contact with the figure that called itself, 'Both'. Its voice could be heard inside of Franklin's head, but neither its mouth moved nor posture changed. Franklin heard him speak almost as an auditory hallucination. Franklin was on such high alert that his heart felt like it would explode through his chest cavity. A heightened sense of desperation and fear cloaked him like warm garments.

"To what extent are the choices?" Franklin asked.

"They are not mine to make," Both continued. "They are simply yours to be measured in the not-so-distant future. It is not effect that is more important than its cause, but if it is "*cause*" that procures effect then what "*cause*" will you intersperse."

Both slowly waved its hand in the air. Suddenly, the winds hushed to almost a complete whisper, and the gloaming landscape surrounding them transposed into an office room. Franklin was astounded by the action. Now within four walls he was surrounded by plaques, furniture, and easy lighting instead of wailing voices and total darkness. Franklin recognized the newly formed space. It was now an image of his father's office presented before him. Franklin gushed over the mesmerizing transformation.

However, within the scene they were not alone. Manifestations of Arthur Mitchell and Jacob Maxwell Sr. stood within the space. The two men argued with each other in a very loud and demonstrative way.

"Arthur, I think it's quite clear what needs to happen here," Maxwell Sr. professed. "I don't want to strong arm you here, but I am simply saying that it is time for the firm to move in a different direction. All of our directors agree that Franklin hasn't met expectations for quite some time.

He must go Arthur.

"He's done excellent work for us in the past, but this Algieri deal could just as well fall through his hands and into another firm's hands. We aren't the only big fish in the pond anymore. Mr. Algieri and his company's business is definitely what this firm needs as a client. Also, as well as those that will follow within that space."

"Jacob, I understand it quite clearly," Arthur responded. "I built this firm from the ground up. Along with your father's sale of his company and Leonard's help all of this has been quite good to my family.

"My life has seen plenty of triumphs, and my wins have come at the expense of many. I found it enjoyable at times to win. It brought about a certain satisfaction to conquer and build by destroying my competition, but frankly I never wanted this for Franklin.

"It can be a beautiful life as a financial advisor or executive sure, but I've seen a great many of men fall prey to jealousy, immorality, and viciousness. At one point I believed myself to be one of them.

"I used to try and shield Franklin from it, but I ultimately failed at that. I wanted more for him. I see that it was wishful thinking to shield him from the happenings in this industry. Lord knows he always had the potential though. But the more I wanted to scare him from it then the more it emblazoned him to prove me otherwise. That's the catch twenty-two.

"He wanted to be his old man. He wanted to beat the old man he had trouble understanding. I would tell him he would never be like me because I truly never wanted him to be. The cynical, greedy, and obnoxious man amplified by his ambition and desires to win at any cost.

"This industry did not change me this way. My ability to always put myself before anything or anyone else did that. To some extent you should improve and grow yourself, but not at the detriment of others. I could have forced him out a long time ago, but then what a disservice would I have done to this firm?

"What a disservice it would have been to our industry? He's always had the drive this firm needs. Always had the focus, but I stifled him at every turn….so what options do I have now?"

Mr. Maxwell continued after a pronounced sigh, "Listen, your retirement is knocking at the door, Arthur. Franklin belongs here, but something must be done to reassure confidence in leadership. I can talk to the partners, but there will be only one exception I think they will find reasonable. You must replace him with Jacob Jr. on the Algieri deal.

"Give it to Junior since he has more experience and specializes in that field. I'm sure the board will find logic in the decision, and they will see it to be fair. It's the only way to salvage it, Arthur. You do that or you might want to prepare yourself for a buyout. In the end it's simple math, Artie. He's not aggressive enough don't you understand! He's the key to your entire legacy. Side by side with Jacob's track record it's clear to see who is far more superior."

The office shifted as Franklin, a bewildered onlooker, stood quietly. Franklin was helpless as Both continued puppeteering the vision before him.

"Swap the account over to Jacob, Franklin gets to stay, and you retire within the year," Mr. Maxwell advised. "Your legacy will be in place and untarnished by a silly buyout. In addition, I will make sure the partners agree to the decision.

"Leave on your own terms. Don't chance your lasting legacy with the firm by having an overly sentimental heart. I would do the same thing if Jacob was in Franklin's shoes. You have to do this. We must make an example that Mitchell, Leonard, and Maxwell demands results, and is always building upon the future. That is whether family is directly involved or not. Franklin, will never have what you have, Artie. He never had the sheer tenacity to grow and build as you have had."

Looking into his scotch glass, Arthur took another sip of the peaty liquid. He then glanced back at Jacob Sr. with a vacant stare.

"So, this is what it comes down to," Arthur said quietly. "I guess that's it then."

The vision then vanished from view as the atmosphere shifted once again. Fury flashed within Franklin's half-lidded eyes. Nothing he could have said would have been more descriptive of his feelings. His mouth became pinched between his teeth and his veins pulsated throughout his neck.

Chapter XXIII

In the end we'll all become stories.

"THAT LYING OLD BASTARD ACTUALLY persuaded my father to agree to that?!!" Franklin thundered. "He made my father choose between firing me or retirement??!! My father would have never taken the Algieri deal away if it wasn't for a phony buyout threat??!! That awful bastard! *DANIEL, CHARLIE*, or whoever you claim to be, I want this to be over! Isn't that a choice? HOW DO I GET OUT OF HERE?!"

"Your presence here is of your own volition Franklin,"

Both stated. "So, therefore, it will be by your own volition that you be removed. It has always been that simple for man. However, the easiest choices to make are never the right ones. Are they?"

Suddenly, the figure named Both vanished into a billow of obscurity.

"WAIT!!" Franklin pleaded.

Franklin was trapped back inside a chaotic scene. The conditions were far worse. A torrential storm of wind and water poured down from the sky as he had been transferred back onto the pathway from before. The gusts of wind and water made it hard for him to maintain footing in the terrifying event.

Flashes of white streaks in the grey skies were the only access to light in the vast darkness. The screams and moans had begun again. The sounds grew louder and could still be heard echoing loudly over the destructive winds. Franklin struggled to find cover from the unyielding storm.

He wanted to run but he could hardly see through the drowning overcast. He covered his face to shield himself from the whipping wind as he thought of a plan. Then he just ran as fast as he could in the direction of a nearby drop-off that wasn't clear to him before. He was running toward it so fast that he nearly plummeted over the descent once he reached it. He caught his balance just before its edge.

He gazed down at a boisterous sea rising and pounding the stone ledge one hundred feet below. Turbulent and unforgiving, the sea crashed and boomed monstrous waves against the rocks at the bottom.

Franklin's eyes widened in disbelief as he looked closer. He had found the source of the screams and wails. He'd heard the sounds carrying over the wind. Over the ledge down below were ghastly creatures that mirrored human bodies.

Chills rolled down Franklin's spine as the noises seemed to grow louder. He slapped his bare hands against his ears to block out the shrill yelping, but it helped him none. He stepped away from the cliff's edge slowly in terror and shock. Then quickly he turned and darted away from the precipice in the opposite direction. As he ran, he couldn't think or anticipate what could be next. His mind was wrecked. His thoughts tossed around in his head like a High Bounce Ball.

Subsequently, in the distance he could see something flickering brightly. It resembled a beam of light or fire. It was a few yards up ahead, but off of the indistinct pathway. Franklin was drawn to its glowing majesty like a moth to flame. He could not resist the urge of an up-close glimpse.

Finally, after fighting through the winds and rain just a short distance more, he arrived at its position. He approached with caution, and he slowly circled around it. At first glance it was frightening to see. Vertically affixed to some sort of stake was a lifeless body. It appeared lifelike just like the creatures in the sea. The imagery of it filled the pit of his stomach with fear. An intense blaze burned the entire fixture from the inside out. With its eyes and mouth wide, Franklin could feel the flame's intensity. The blaze raged immensely even as the rain persisted.

However, as hot as the seething flame was it did not burn or destroy the outside of the body. The fiery combustion maintained itself internally without ever harming it externally.

'What was this with searing red flames for eyes, and held within the middle of this chaos? How was the flame still burning?' Franklin thought to himself.

For a better vantage point, Franklin loomed nearer to examine the fixture closer. Through the overcast, the features of it looked somewhat familiar. To his dismay it was an effigy of himself. It was Franklin! As the flames continued to glow from the body he could not turn away from the heap. He became disoriented by what he saw. Panic took a tight grasp of his limbs without any signs of letting go.

Franklin eased away gingerly before his speed increased to a full sprint. He tripped himself up as he turned to view the glowing pyre behind. Lying flat on the ground he face palmed. He was alone in a place he was unfamiliar with and afraid of. The darkness consumed his form. No one was there to help rescue him from the ongoing havoc he was witnessing. It was just him.

He curled up on the black and brown disintegrated granular. Franklin was beginning to give up. Fear and hopelessness filled his heart. The man was now filled with anguish.

“WHAT DO YOU WANT FROM ME?!!” Franklin hollered.

His voice seemed to echo over the winds. He had the same fright as an unsuspecting insect caught in a spider’s web. Unexpectedly, the rain and whipping winds began to cease its onslaught to a peaceful serenity. Instantly all of the noise and bombardment of the wind and rain attack was over. Franklin’s body was bruised and chaffed from the storm. He was extremely fatigued and weak. Alone and disconnected from all things familiar to him he had now reached a breaking point. Then Franklin felt a hand touch his shoulder.

He peered up and around from his fetal position, and noticed someone or something standing in front of him.

Unlike the mysterious man from earlier on, this figure did not have a congenial appearance.

His eyes upwardly scanned the figure's anatomy slowly. From the ground it was difficult to identify who or what the figure was that stood before him. It had hands and it had feet that resembled a human body. Taking what strength he had left, Franklin grabbed the figure's hand and lifted himself up.

He was too far removed and too unaware of time and space. He had no idea how long he had been in this disastrous place or for how much longer he would be there. That was until he saw him. Franklin's eyes gleamed as recognition covered his face. If only for a brief while his hopelessness had suddenly evaporated.

The presence and energy of this figure was enough to jolt the dead back to life. It was enough for Franklin to gather belief there was meaning behind all of this. The belief for which this affliction was only temporary and not some beginning to other hardships. Gazing at the figure's face he was almost frozen where he stood.

Although the pathway was still dark ahead, the tint from the figure lit up the area surrounding them both. It was not human, but in human form. The figure was emitting a glow from all over its being. The glow was as beautiful as the horizon at golden hour.

The garb upon it was of a sparkling white greyish coloring. Judging by its length it could have covered Franklin from his neck to his feet. The figure's appearance was beyond classically beautiful as well. The undeniable exuberance in its features were captivating and remarkable.

"Hello," the figure said in a low dramatic tone.

"Pop?!!" Franklin exclaimed. Bliss filled his heart. An intense stream of tears flowed down Franklin's cheeks as he gripped ahold of the embodiment.

Embracing the figure, his grasp was one he did not want to break in fear that he might be left alone yet again. The figure was indeed Arthur's spiritual being standing before him.

"Dad, I'm so sorry," Franklin muttered. "I never knew about Jacob and his plan! Why didn't you tell me? I never knew it! I should've known about the way you truly felt! My own ambitions and hatred for you clouded me! I didn't get it pop, and I'm sorry for everything. I'm so sorry. I was stupid, young, and angry!"

"Son, all is forgiven for those who forgive themselves and others," the embodiment replied. "I love you too, and what's done is done. You must have no concern of it now. All things have happened and will always happen by the action of our discretion. You must only concern yourself with the matters in which you can change now."

"Wait a minute!" Franklin insisted.

He swallowed hard before speaking again, "How did you get here?"

Franklin's chest rose and fell in rapid breaths. He tensed the figure's shoulders as he grabbed both of them tightly.

Arthur's embodiment gave a gentle smile before it replied, "Son there isn't much for what was at this current moment. This is all that's left of a man who lived his life, and now must answer for the way it was lived. Choices made not too long ago must be answered for. There is no one to save anyone from their own comeuppance but themselves. That is what you must learn if nothing else."

Franklin gave his father's being a chilling look as the winds began to pick up speed again. The embodiment's glow commenced to dim out within the darkness of the atmosphere.

"Wait a minute!" Franklin fretted. "POP, WAIT! Don't leave me here please! I don't understand what you mean!"

"Find what's missing, Franklin," the being said. "Take the path that leads in, and you will find what will lead you out."

"What am I looking for?" Franklin boomed. "Where does the path lead to?"

The rain started to shower the desolate tract once more as Arthur's fading projection spoke a familiar name. The name startled Franklin into an immediate torment.

"Dani," the figure spoke again. "Find your way, and you both will find each other!"

"Pop?!" Franklin shouted. "POP?!!"

Franklin's body went limp. He rubbed his temple softly as his gaze fell to his feet.

As quickly as the being had appeared on the pathway it left just as fast. If Franklin was no closer to comprehension of what was happening before then he surely was no closer to clarity afterwards. All he knew was that he wanted out. From the looks of things, the only way out was taking the path that lied before him. If what the being said was true then his daughter was trapped in the *In Between* too. Franklin had no other options but to push forward. The way in led to the way out.

Chapter XXIV

Understanding is an art, and not everyone is an artist.

DENISE SAT ALONE QUIETLY INSIDE THE hospital chapel. She was well aware of her son and granddaughter's plight. They would be facing many tests up ahead. She knew exactly what was about to transpire in some faraway place. She knew that Franklin and Dani's comas would only be overcome if they could overcome the challenges Daniel set before them both. Somewhere not of this world their characters would be tested. The timeline of these events had been set in motion some time long before they ever were a thought. Denise sat beside Vivienne as she sat quietly in the chapel too. Denise knew her daughter-in-law needed all the support she could handle and then some.

The two women sat there in the old stone and stained-glass prayer room. The quiet air was filled with the fragrancy of a gentle nature scent. It emitted from incense and candles meticulously organized throughout the room. The votive arrangements surrounding them did their best to mask the fetor from the fusty old prayer books stored inside.

Despite the faint malodorous smell, it was a beautiful place to pray and cogitate. Vivienne appeared to be in a trance by the blank stare overlaying her face. She leaned forward and clutched her hands underneath her chin. Denise's eyes fixated heavenward as she held her hands tightly clasped in her lap. Her eyes bore into the vaulted ceiling as she whispered a prayer.

"Denise, what exactly did you mean the other day?" Vivienne asked.

She was still looking straight ahead toward the front of the chapel.

"You know when you said 'I thought we had more time.' What did that mean?"

"Vivienne, I was referring to Arthur, Franklin, and I," Denise stated. "I was the only person that knew Arthur was sick. It hurts me to know that the last part of Arthur's life was spent in an ugly spot with Franklin.

"He did not want anyone to know of his illness, but I believe if Franklin had known then things would've been different. However, keeping everyone in the dark were his wishes so I followed them. When I said he said "We had more time' I was referring to a simple fact. That was once Arthur's prognosis was given we had made a pact that we would spend as much time together as we could.

"He made a promise to me he wanted to keep but couldn't. I just always trusted in Arthur to make things right. However, we must deal with the hands we are given."

Denise exhaled before she turned to ask Vivienne her most important question, "How are you holding up?"

"I don't really know how to feel to be honest Denise," Vivienne asserted. "I just don't know what to think since there is a strong chance that they may not make it. I keep asking myself how he didn't see the deer in the road.

"It was so horrific and split-second. Now I'm even more at a loss for words since Arthur's death. This has been the craziest week of my life and I'm hoping it's all just a dream. It's not though"

A deafening silence filled the chapel again as the two ladies meditated on the situation. Vivienne wallowed in her doubt. Her confidence was nearly gone, and every second took its toll on her psyche. The days were becoming grimmer as time passed. Her stomach had been in a knot for so long it's as if her abdomen had become a human sized twist tie.

Staying strong for herself, Franklin, Danielle, and now Mrs. Mitchell weighed heavily on her. She hadn't slept soundly in days, but they would have to drag her away to keep her from her family.

Chapter XXV

Right now, what do you want out of life?

DENISE NOTICED THE TEARS BUILDING IN Vivienne's eyes. Breaking the short silence, she began to speak, "I've had more than my fair share of tragedies, Vivienne. Maybe a little bit more than I expected earlier on, but I've felt the same feelings you feel now. *Exactly how you feel*!"

The color drained out of Vivienne's face as she studied Mrs. Mitchell closely. She sat back on the wooden pew.

"How do you mean, Denise?" Vivienne asked.

Sadness clouded Denise's features. She twisted her wedding ring around on her finger.

"Well, some time ago even before Franklin was born, I had to overcome a great disaster that occurred in my life," Denise lamented. "Arthur was a good man deep within his heart, and although, he wasn't perfect, he was mine."

"Years ago, I lost someone else that meant the world to me. I lost a beautiful little an—"

"Mrs. Mitchell?" a soft voiced interrupted from behind.

Both of the Mitchell women answered in their bright harmonious voices, " *YES*?"

It was Dani's friends from school. Monica and Emma stood together in the chapel aisle. The two young ladies hadn't seen Dani since the day of the accident. The volleyball tournament had started and they dedicated winning their first game to her.

"Girls!" Vivienne gushed. "I'm so happy to see you two. How are you both?!"

"We're fine under the circumstances," Monica encouraged. "Both Emma and I wanted to come by and see Dani. Also, we wanted to thank you for allowing us to visit with her today."

"We definitely did not want to impose on the family's privacy," Emma added. "Hello, Nana Mitchell. So, good to see you as well! It's been a long time."

"Hello, ladies," Denise said. "It's so nice to see you both again. It has been quite some time, but both of you have grown to be so beautiful. Haven't they, Vivienne? They're so adorable!"

"They truly have grown," Vivienne agreed. "Plus, Emma you two are never imposing at all. Dani has known you both forever, and you're both considered family. She would be happy you both visited her."

Vivienne's soft-spoken words triggered deep emotions in the eldest of the two young women. Monica could no longer hold back her grief. She no longer had control of the dam she built up to restrict any visible anguish. The strength it took to remain supportive was now too much to maintain on her own. The barrier deep within her heart had broken. Her sadness could no longer be contained or suppressed. A river of tears flowed freely down her cheeks.

"We app—we appreciate that Mrs. Mitchell," Monica responded. "Dani means the world to us."

She covered her face with her hands.

"I know," Vivienne replied. She embraced Monica tightly. "It's going to be okay. I promise."

Vivienne held Monica close. Monica sunk into the warmth of Vivienne's body. Vivienne's embrace made her feel less glum.

Monica's voice trembled as she spoke up again, "She's the only family we both have! Blood or not. It's been very tough not seeing her at school, and not hearing her voice."

Emma entwined herself around Vivienne and Monica as Denise looked on.

"It's been really hard, Mrs. Mitchell," Emma echoed. "It's been all over the news too. Not seeing her at practice or in class has had me so worked up. It's been very hard to manage knowing she's in here. Monica and I told each other we did not want to come here until we had our emotions in check, but we we're fooling ourselves. Even though it's hard, we still want to be super strong for her, Mrs. Mitchell."

"I know, Emma," Vivienne comforted. "Danielle would be happy to know you both are here. Don't cry. I don't want all three of my girls in pain. It's going to be okay. Isn't that right, Denise?"

Denise rose from her seat. She stood tall and showed no weakness.

"That's right, girls!" Denise guaranteed. "This is a very emotional time, but to know you both care so much for her speaks volumes in itself! Hang tough and hang tight! Dani and her father will pull through this with the love we all have for them!"

Monica and Emma inched forward to bring Denise into the group hug.

"Well, ladies shall we go up?" Vivienne asked.

"We're ready when you are, Mrs. Mitchell," Emma confirmed.

"Let's go," Vivienne said. "Denise, are you coming along?"

"No, I think I will stay here for a bit," Denise stated. "You all go on ahead. I'll be up soon. It was so good to see you ladies! Both of you have grown up to be so gorgeous. I love it!"

"Thank you, Mrs. Mitchell," both ladies chorused. "We'll see you upstairs."

"Do you need anything, Denise?" Vivienne asked.

Denise sat back down on the wooden bench and replied, "No. I'm fine. I'll be up in a bit. I'll see you later girls."

Vivienne and the two young ladies made their way out of the chapel. They left Denise behind. Instantaneously Mrs. Mitchell received a text message from Mrs. Rearden that read:

'Hello. Denise, I hope things are better for you today than they have been. I wanted to message you to let you know that Jacob is making a serious push to become the CEO and Chairman of the board after Arthur's passing. It seems likely that he could get it because I know for sure he has a strong influence within the board.'

'I also hear he will motion that you be bought out so that there are no roadblocks to get in his way. The board meeting will still be as scheduled. It is now my belief that "Investor confidence" is his main edge moving forward. Since you were the TOD beneficiary and I anticipate Jacob to exercise all means.... he may make it very ugly.'

The text message could have been reason to panic, but it was a move by Jacob that Denise was anticipating. Since the company had gone public, Arthur's estate plan had been revised and updated constantly. It allowed a huge percent of his interests and shares to transfer to Denise upon his death.

At the moment she was the acting CEO and Chairman of the board. Arthur also had a very precise will in place that put a substantial amount of earnings in a trust for Franklin's benefit at the time of his death.

In addition, another percent of his interests was to transfer to Franklin to avoid probate. If there was one great defining characteristic of Arthur Mitchell, just one, then it was his ability to anticipate every move and a counter to it. He never spent much of his time defending his stakes, but rather attacking his opposition's stake constantly.

His type of diligence and ingenuity was something hard to find in the likes of his contemporaries. He also had an abundance of contingencies. He had a 'wild card' in Denise no one knew about. In case the Maxwell's really put up a fight for dominance within the firm, he was prepared for that fight. He feared there would be a power struggle, but he spent most of his last years planning for it.

Many nights Arthur would coach up Denise on the ins and outs of the business. After years of his coaching, she was ready to continue his legacy. No one would be bullying her around. She was always a leader and CEO. She was Arthur's very own personal one. While he was the corporate CEO of Mitchell, Leonard, and Maxwell, she was Arthur's "Chief Emotional Officer" at home. During the years he spent building the business, she knew he would need the support.

As the years of their marriage continued to add on, she was there to provide Arthur with moral strength and any support necessary to combat the high stress environment he was in. She saw what the industry was all about. She had heard the stories. She witnessed some of the savagery firsthand.

Already she was a good listener by nature and it provided her with the ability to offer constant perspective. She brought a balance into Arthur's life that didn't allow him to get too high or ever too low.

If Maxwell Sr.'s influence was what Mrs. Rearden feared then Mrs. Rearden would be more than happy with the type of influence Denise had. Denise had resiliency even in the face of her momentary personal catastrophes.

Her resolve was unmatched when it came to identifying the character of people. She always knew to beware of the Maxwells. Plus, Arthur made her aware of all his cronies within the firm. Arthur nor his wife were foolish enough to think the Maxwells wouldn't eventually want "*GET BACK*" after he took over the elder Maxwell's company.

He knew if there would be any legacy of his to continue then Denise would have to fight to secure it. She would have to fight to maintain their family involvement moving forward.

Denise represented both a role model and a provider of substantive mentoring. She would be the perfect successor to Arthur's historic run. This was all Arthur's imagining as he wrote out his will. He knew without question that her passion and guts were equal to only a hunting honey badger.

From the outside, some would question her qualifications, but she didn't mind it. With Arthur gone and Franklin in his uncertain condition, she knew they would question any plans of continued success. It didn't matter though. She knew upon taking helm of the company it would bring along its challenges and challengers. Although her background was not one of financial services, she was equipped with the leadership, awareness, and emotional calm it took to assume the role of CEO.

For years spending her time as an anesthesiologist, she developed and crafted supreme patience and attention to detail. The proud matriarch finally rose from the pew to leave from the chapel.

As the entrance of the chapel came into sight, her thoughts began to drift into a daze. Denise froze in the middle of the aisle. She shifted from one foot to the other from what she envisioned from memory. Her eyes widened as an old moment in time spilled out of her mind. It was if she were no longer in the present, but somehow taken back to a day when all her troubles, her worries, and fears were non-existent.

She harkened back deep into her memory. The room no longer smelled of candles and incense or faint molder. It was no longer stark and monochromatic but now vibrant and lively. The room was full and bright now. Denise was caught within a daydream of something festive.

Standing at the entrance of the chapel she could see her younger self. In her early twenties, with high cheekbones, almond shaped eyes, and jet-black hair flowing down and below her shoulders, she was lovely to look at. The young featly Denise captivated the room of onlookers standing around her. She was wearing a lovely wedding gown. The memory of that day was still as vivid as the moment it happened. The young Denise walked down the aisle of the chapel in her cream-colored gown made of soft satin fabric. Like a lover's lips, the gown kissed her body perfectly. As lightly as a gymnast, she strolled past her spectating loved ones.

A young Arthur Mitchell gazed at his soon to be bride from the front of the chapel. The young up and coming financial advisor was ready to give his soon to be wife anything she asked for. His entire face was lit up from ear to ear. Their marriage had been inevitable from the time they were in college together. They were both the center of each other's universe.

For a brief moment Denise was lost in the memory of one her life's happiest moments. She could even remember what she told her young husband on that day exactly. With her eyes closed she mouthed the words:

"Arthur, I pledge to care and love you until the day I die. To be worthy of your love is the greatest gift I could've asked for on this day. I promise to be patient, honest, kind, and forgiving no matter what storm may come. Unconditionally, I promise to love you without reservation, and comfort you in times of distress. To laugh with you and cry with you are lifetime endeavors because I pledge to never leave your side.

"I will forever make every effort to remain your best friend, counselor, consoler, and navigator. To stray from you would mean that you are not the compass I believe you to be but you indeed are! So, if ever you or I should get lost or tumble in this beautiful thing called life, I want you to know that I will be a beacon shining bright for each of us to find our way again. I love you so much on this day and will forever. My love is constant, and will not ever change."

Joy enraptured the features of Denise's face as she finished. The young Denise's vows were enough to move even the apathetic to tears. Then the young Arthur's words to her were just as profound and poignant to such a degree that tears welled into the eyes of the older Denise. She remembered him say:

"Denise, everyone has their own motivations to get up in the morning and face the day, but you have always been my motivation. Today I want you to know that there is no one who can ever replace you. I think back to the first time I laid eyes on you, and I knew right then that I had found someone incredible. Ever since that very moment all I have ever wanted was to be with you. I fought for you! I fought hard to be worthy of your love!

"As I see you each day no matter how dark my day might be, it always makes me realize that being with you makes it worthwhile. You are my light! You are my vision!

You are my inspiration! I looked forward to this day to reassure you of something and that is to say my love is eternal. It won't bend, it won't break, and it won't fold! I will do whatever it takes to keep you wanting to keep me! My love has no beginning Denise, and it has no end. In life and in death it is and will always be forever. I love you and will cherish you all the days of my life."

Arthur's pronouncement was a deafening confirmation of the love he had for his bride. His intention was to stick by her side for the long haul, and through whatever challenge. His love for Denise was not something concocted or contrived. It was something he felt deep down within his soul. On that day a bond was cemented. Mrs. Mitchell knew she was willing to fight through anything to keep her marriage together too.

She meant every word of her vows. Even when Arthur admitted to what he knew was the truth surrounding their firstborn's death. Still, she never left his side. She remained devoted to an oath. She remained devoted to him. But it would be too cookie cutter to think her reaction was not complete shock and disbelief.

'*This story he told her could not have been real life.*' She remembers thinking.

It was a truly unbelievable story. At first it only upset Denise that it borderline insulted her intellectually. It was hard to imagine Arthur had unwittingly altered their lives by a response to a question from some mysterious man in a hospital lobby. That was until that mysterious man showed up to meet her too. The manifestation they knew as Charlie and Daniel appeared to them as he had in many other forms to people since and before.

With Arthur's one knee-jerk reaction it displayed a vulnerability within him. Although he was a man filled with virtue, respect, and dignity, he too like many others believed money could fix everything. The response depicted a man not as confident in himself internally as he displayed externally.

His response to the figure known as Charlie was one filled with fear and a misconception. Although money is nice to have when you need it, it doesn't necessarily bring happiness. Most of all Denise didn't care if they lived in a cardboard box so long as they had each other. She was never in love with him for the money or material possessions.

She married Arthur, the man she believed in. Although they struggled at first, she knew he was on the precipice of something great. He never could be categorized as just some struggling financial advisor with his head in the clouds. Not to her. She loved her husband through those trials just as much if not more when she recited the words, "I do".

Even after knowing all that, she knew she still did not blame Arthur for any of it. Things happened for a reason she believed. That's the way she carried around the tragedy of losing her first born, Danielle, all these years.

As the daydream of her wedding day faded and reality set back in, she noticed she was still standing in the chapel aisle. Other people had filed inside by then.

She proceeded toward the exit swiftly. A new focus had energized her. She was galvanized to conquer the unknown. If Jacob Maxwell was ready for a fight, then she was ready too.

Chapter XXVI

"Real" isn't who's with you at a celebration,

"Real" is who's standing next to you when you hit rock bottom.

FRANKLIN'S MIND RACED. HE WAS STILL running on the long endless path. He tried to absorb all that was told to him by his father. How any of this was real and not just some crazy nightmare was still a question in his mind. Time seemed to drag beyond a normality in the *In Between.*

'*How could it be? Was the figure he saw truly his father?*

Was he truly of this world now? How was any of it possible?' He asked himself.

It was pitch dark and he could barely see the pathway he was tasked to follow. Flashes of lightning lit up the dark skies every few seconds. They illuminated his placement. The rain fell in torrents as it continued. Agitation of the land made Franklin's feet sink deeper with every footfall. No matter how fast he ran it still felt like he wasn't getting anywhere. He could not see far out in front of him, and he could not outpace the sheets of beating rain against his body.

Suddenly, the path of loose rock and mud began winding around a rocky ledge of a steep decline. Franklin's next steps had begun curling downward. To his right he could then see the spectacular sea of bodies once more. The horrid screams filled the cavities of his ears with every step forward he took. Peering out towards the outlining sea, thousands upon thousands of human sized beings were moaning and gnashing away at each other. The horrific scene captivated Franklin. The subjects shrilled loudly with great pain and suffering as lightning continued to illuminate the skies overhead.

In the distance he could see a small craft crossing the sea. It moved slowly across the water as the ghastly beings tried to reach into its rickety wooden frame. He was frozen in place by the frightening sight.

He could see other strange looking subjects of various description seated on the vessel as it crossed. Beyond the capsule there was this great wall. It towered across on the other side of the sea. It seemed to be the vessel's destination. Gagging and almost near vomiting by the sight and smells, Franklin looked away and continued moving further down the path. Although he could barely see each step-in front of him, he kept pace along the rocky mountainside. He held onto the rocky wall to his left for balance and support.

At the very bottom of the rocky decline, he could see another small light breaking through the darkness. It grew larger as he proceeded. It seemed to be a huge opening of some sort down below. Franklin picked up his pace. Finally, he came to an entrance. It was what appeared to be a tunnel. The area on the other side was lit better than the one he was in currently. Again, he approached slightly. Hesitation to go through it proved harder to overcome than he thought it would be before.

There was wording written above the doorway. He could not read it of course. It was in a language he could not decipher. He shuddered before taking in a sharp breath. He built the courage and finally took action by going through the short burrow to the other side. As he exited the tunnel on the opposite end a magnificent plain came into view. The atmosphere was calmer but cloudy. There was no rain pouring down in thunderous waves, nor any winds whooshing across the land. The skyline was lined with clouds as far as Franklin could see, and provided just enough lighting to view the landscape in its entirety. Though somewhere in the distance he could still hear the anguish of soft screams on the other side.

In every direction there were male and female beings scattered all over. They came across as not having a care or sense of each other, but others wandered around speaking incoherently to themselves. Franklin tried stopping one of the individuals to get information about their location. Up closer, a man was sobbing profusely. Heavy-set with short wide legs, the man moved in great haste. He had red blisters and sores all over his body.

Franklin slapped a hand over his mouth at the sight of the injuries.

“Excuse me,” he pressed. “Hey, excuse me! What is this place? Where are we?!”

The man never showed Franklin any attention as walked on. The man just continued to ramble to himself without any interruption. It was as if he didn’t notice Franklin standing there at all. As Franklin watched the man plod away, he was approached by someone else.

“Don’t mind him,” a stranger said. “He can neither see nor hear you. It is not because he does not have eyes or ears. It is because his concerns are focused upon his judgement.”

The stranger’s face was mostly shrouded by an unkempt beard that clung to his skin like winter ravaged rose tendrils.

“Who are you?” Franklin questioned. “Can you help me find a way out of here? I need to know where the way out is.”

“So, you are looking for a way out?” the stranger asked. “Well, the way in is always the way out. However, I find it necessary for you to ask yourself a question first. Why are you here to begin with?”

Franklin’s face contorted. He hung his head in confusion.

“Aren’t you also looking for someone?” the stranger asked.

Franklin’s head whipped back up at attention.

“Where is she?!” Franklin demanded. “Danielle? Where is she?!”

“I saw her,” the stranger confessed. “But she is no longer here. She has left this place to meet the ferryman, and he is beyond this level.”

"Level?" Franklin puzzled. "Can you take me to her?"

"She spoke unto me about you," the stranger said. "It is my own understanding that she is aware of your presence here and has chosen to search for you too."

"TAKE ME TO HER!" Franklin insisted.

He laid his hands on the stranger's shoulders as he continued, "Can you take me to her? PLEASE? I have to find her! She is my daughter."

"Are you sure *she* is the reason why you are here?" the stranger asked. "You are unaware of where you are, and what this place is. But this place knows who you are, and of your presence too. Frank—"

"How do you know my name?" Franklin asked.

"Franklin, the *In Between* is a place of the dead. Although you are among the dead, you are not dead. Yet here you are standing before me. Where is your daughter? Well, the answer to that question will be answered in time. However, you must answer another question first. Why are you here?

"Although the person you seek is faraway, she is closer now than the shadow of your being. She has chosen to go across with the ferryman to a place where the living cannot enter. She is neither dead nor alive in this place, but her worldly body is weak and close to letting go if—"

"IF WHAT?" Franklin exclaimed.

Suddenly, Franklin noticed something over the stranger's shoulder. He glanced out beyond the horizon. He could now see that what he thought were clouds in the sky were something else entirely. Chaos ensued among the scattered individuals roaming around the plain. The mock clouds started to descend to the land.

The masses brought with them a dreadful buzzing sound that was very distinct. It echoed all over the moor.

Franklin recognized what it was. The mock clouds were swarms of hornets and other insects. Panic made Franklin lose his grip. Fight or flight gripped his mind. Instantly in one fell swoop the swarm began viciously attacking the crowd. The swarms hovered over and around all of them. Screams intensified as the insects stung the subjects. The noise and confusion filled the environment with a deafening sound.

Everyone ran and ran all over the plain, but the insects did not tire. At the feet of the crowd worms erupted from the soil feasting on the tears and blood of the despaired. The slimy earthworms did not come within a few feet of Franklin or the stranger's feet. It was if the stranger and he were protected from the invertebrate and horde of hornets.

"What's happening?!" Franklin shrieked.

Tears began to shimmer in his eyes as the subject's screams continued. He trembled at the event taking place. Franklin grabbed ahold of the stranger again.

"We have to get out of here before they attack us too!" Franklin shouted. "Do you not know the way out of here?! Can't you help them?"

"Calm yourself, Franklin," the stranger said. "You will not be harmed. But if you need a guide out then I will lead you. However, no one here can escape. It is the reason why they scatter. They will wander all over this moor into perpetuity. Their improvidence is their punishment forever.

"The uncommitted of those who chose not to choose, those who chose neither to rebel nor pledge themselves to one side or another will always reside here. They will wallow here in agony and regret of indecision. In the *In Between* there is not one. One must choose wisely between what is pure and what is impure, but choose they must. The choice of indecision, of faith and allegiance to either side, is now their detriment.

"Choice will always be the foundation of one's own misery or happiness. This plain is filled with those who could not see past their own neutrality or themselves. However, do not fret for their fate is not yours if you do not wish it to be. Opportunity has not forsaken you—yet. Your journey is not finished. The path lies uncreated."

Franklin fell to his knees. In that very moment a deep sorrow overtook the middle-aged man's heart. The corners of his eyes crinkled. He had begun to think back to a conversation he had with his mother some time ago. He remembered what he had said to her. He didn't believe in any of these things. Good or bad. The righteous or unrighteous. He could have cared less.

Franklin did not believe in such a world or place for the dead. Since childhood he had not believed in such a place where punishment awaited those who exhibited the ways the stranger spoke of. The news of this was met with absolute incredulity. As an adult he did not partake in the belief that there was some ultimate judgement in the hereafter that determined one's fate based on the choices he or she made.

He wept on his knees as he began to question his actions and belief of what he was witnessing. Bewailing continued to temper the air.

'How could any of it be real or feel real?' He pondered to himself.

He knelt down in the moor thinking on past choices

he'd made that could have led him to the *In Between.*

"If I am not dead here then what am I here?" asked Franklin. "I can still smell, hear, and touch things, but not in the ways I once did. I feel I am not of blood and bone anymore but of something else. Upon my arrival here I felt enormous energy. It was like bathing in the pit of the sun. I had an awareness of myself outside of myself and within my psyche I felt emotions all at once. Rage, grief, sorrow, and fear all overtook me. I could hear faint sounds ringing in my ears. I heard voices, but I could not answer out to them. I could not move, I could not speak, but I could feel. Then in an absolute flash there was nothingness. Then I saw *Both.*"

Franklin whimpered quietly.

He continued, "You mentioned Danielle left to meet with a ferryman. Where?"

"I know the way to her," the stranger responded. "I can show you the way, but I cannot choose for you to follow."

"Take me to her," Franklin pleaded. "Help me find her."

"I will guide you," the stranger confirmed. "Although it was a very long time ago, I have shown the way before."

Chapter XXVII

People change. Memories don't.

THE STRANGER, NOW FRANKLIN'S GUIDE, reached out his hand to pick him up from the sediment. He began walking ahead of him on what was now a visible course. The earthworms dispersed with each footfall they made. Franklin tried hard not to feel any way about anything he'd seen so far but the feeling of guilt was overpowering him. He turned away from it all in shame. Walking along the path, his new guide began to speak openly with Franklin.

"The young woman in which you call your daughter has an honest soul," the guide declared. "She is unlike most of those I have encountered. She knows the true meanings of sacrifice, forgiveness, and humility. She said many great things about your family, but she was also very discouraged and weary."

"How so?" Franklin queried.

"I am curious to know what it is that you believe Franklin," replied the guide.

Franklin cowered at the comment.

He started again, "I haven't been the best father to her. I haven't been the best husband or son for that matter either. I have been so consumed with my own endeavors that everyone else hasn't mattered much to me in such a long time.

"I made up in my mind that I would focus on my own goals and getting even with my father rather than spend time nurturing relationships with my family. I made terrible choices in that regard. I placed many tangible things above nobility and righteousness.

"My ambition to outdo my father was my driving force. I was and have always been fueled by my hurt and anger. So, I can understand Dani's disappointment in me. But that's the thing about her—she's not like me. She's not like anyone in our family. She doesn't hold grudges or wait for the '*get back*'.

"She's a great friend and person. I don't think anyone could outdo her in that category. She's kind, and she's forgiving. No matter how many times you wrong her she still stands and fights hard for you."

"Would you admit to having taken advantage of those characteristics that make her who she is Franklin," the guide asked.

"I cannot deny that I have lied to my daughter on several occasions knowing full well I wouldn't stand by my word or what I had promised. I've treated my wife more as a roommate than the woman I took an oath with.

"I can feel her hurt. It's always written on her face. Do they love me? I am confident that they do, but I know for sure they are not as confident in my word anymore.

"I haven't been the most trustworthy or dependable person over a number of years. My own frustrations from my very own father would be easy to point out. It would be easy to justify what I've done and haven't done, but it was all my choice. I just need them to know that I'm truly sorry. I need for them to know I want to correct my mistakes.

"I waited too late to make things right with my father. Our relationship should've been better. Being stubborn and foolish ruined every opportunity to make things right. I don't want to waste anymore of the time I have with my daughter like I chose to do with my father."

"Franklin, it is true that choice breeds circumstance?" the guide asked. "No reaction can be made without action. It is in a man's heart that which breeds thought. Thought then cultivates action. Therefore, his circumstances are but remnants of what his thoughts are."

The guide and Franklin stopped for a moment. The grief struck Franklin like a blow to the temple. He was assailed by the turmoil he felt. His guilt sank him deeper and deeper into a state of pity. He felt awful for himself.

"Thoughts are seeds sown into the mind with objectives to take root there if allowed," the guide continued. "It blossoms sooner or later into acts which bear opportunity and circumstance. So, you see it is your choice. It is your free will to cultivate whatever you choose. It has been your decision to harness anger against your father which in turn has strained the relationship you have with your very own family."

Suddenly, from the shadows of the terrain a shadowy figure wandered about. It was a male individual scampering in a frenzy. Franklin focused in.

"He is what we call a shade," the guide acknowledged. "A shade is similar to a soul. Every being you see has departed the land of the living into the world of the *In Between* until it is determined where they must go. The living cannot survive here. The dead are the only individuals who can take residence. In this place you are neither, and cannot be harmed."

"So, what am I then?" Franklin asked.

"You are awake," the guide replied.

The shade began to speak to them, "Can you help me? HELP ME, PLEASE! Where am I? I am not supposed to be here! I don't deserve this! Please, help me please?

"You're okay," Franklin said. "What is your name? You can come with us. Can't we help this man? He can get you out of here with us, can't you?"

"NO!" the shade screamed. "I WANT OUT OF HERE NOW! Don't you understand?!"

"Come with us," Franklin started again.

The shade continued to grow more and more disgruntled. He became more combative as the guide and Franklin looked on. The shade had become infuriated with anger.

He unleashed more words of vitriol, "I gave what I could! I helped people that I could've stepped over! Doesn't that mean anything? I gave to charities and foundations all the time. I was awarded 'Philanthropist of the Year' for what I've done!! Is it because I wouldn't give my hard-earned money to every single homeless dirt bag I saw? IS THIS WHAT THIS IS ABOUT?! Those guys didn't deserve anything from me.

"I sinned! So what? But I never murdered anyone. I am a respected man!! Where I'm from I'm a respected man! DO YOU HEAR ME?!! I never murdered anyone! IT'S ALL THAT WHORE'S FAULT!! That dirty skank got me into all of this!"

"William, I must correct you," the guide chimed in. "She did not. She will have her day just as you will have yours. But your choices are of your own."

The shade tried to attack the guide, but could not physically do so. He no longer had control over his frame or movements. Startling enough he began to slowly sink into the ground where he stood.

"What's happening?!" the shade yelled. "WAIT!! Help me!"

The shade descended into the ground like moisture from an overcast. Franklin attempted to pull the man up, but was stopped by his guide. The guide held him back as they both watched the shade helplessly sink. The shade screamed for help that was not coming.

"Listen to me Franklin," the guide said. "This is William and William was certainly not incapable of making the right choices. No one is. William had an abundance of passion and vigor in his lifetime; yet it was not used for good.

"His lapse in judgement and weakness of will has positioned him here. He reveled in fornication and misbehaviors with another on earth. Feel no remorse for him Franklin. Even now he is still convinced he has done no wrong.

"His grotesque obsession for riches, glory, and acknowledgment has consumed him. On earth it is true that his lover's husband killed him. For him that did not allow him any opportunity to repent. For this reason, he is condemned here."

The shade continued screaming as Franklin tried his best to hear what his guide was saying. It took great effort. The shade's screams resembled the screeches of pigs at a slaughter, though Franklin's guide was undeterred or distracted by the wails. The land had not faltered anywhere else except under the shade's feet.

The guide continued on with his oration, "William's passion represents a man whose only concern is for himself and the material things he loves. Not even his soul came before his lust and greed.

"He found his true happiness which is now the bane of his agony. The love of another man's wife and greed of worldly possessions. His love for these trappings were once his Elysium on earth; it will now be his inferno here."

The guide turned to address the shade. He was almost out of view. He could still be seen from the neck up.

"Sinners retain all of the qualities for which they were damned, and they will remain the same throughout perpetuity William," the guide said. "The soul is depicted here with the same distinctive traits that condemned it here in the first place.

"Consequently, as you were truly a greedy adulterer in the human world then throughout eternity you will be chastened as an adulterer."

The shade's entire body had become fully engulfed.

The land had gorged upon him until he was out of sight. The land hardened back to its original state, and both the guide and Franklin continued onward.

Chapter XXVIII

Your salary is the bribe they give you to forget your dreams.

FRANKLIN'S EXPRESSION CLOSED ALL THE way up. He was still reeling and anxious from what just transpired. His guide walked up ahead of him as they moved along.

The guide broke in, "There was once a child in the wilderness who had become separated from his father. His mother and family were in no position to search for him because they too were lost. With nothing to eat or even shelter his head from the rain, he began to remember what lessons his father had taught him. Reflecting on those lessons, his father began to come to him. The child began to hear him speak.

"He had found his father in his heart and thoughts. Albeit in his deep reflection, his father's teachings had never left him. Although he could not see him physically, on the contrary he was with him.

"With those memories of instruction and teachings, the child constructed a makeshift shelter. He was able to also manifest a garden in the middle of the wilderness by learning the land and using what he could find.

"However, his work was not finished. He was still tasked with the garden's cultivation. Although his father's teachings showed him the way, it still was dependent upon the newfound gardener to either cultivate intelligently or let his garden run wild in the wilderness. The child still had a choice. Either tend to the garden in such a way to bring forth a good reaping or face having a bad one.

"Whether he chose to wisely sow and tend to it or not the garden would still produce. Hence, by pursuing and choosing to free the garden from weeds and debris, the gardener recognized his choice operated in the shaping of the garden's overall health, circumstance, and destiny. Cause and effect are as absolute and undeviating in all things as tangible things can be observed with the senses."

The guide paused without saying anything further. He turned and took in the sight of Franklin. The guide had a tired look upon his face as he stood still in the pathway. He analyzed the man's face for any form of positive interpretation.

The guide had been in the *In Between* for a great while. He had shown someone else the deepest parts of the darkened place before. Many moons previously.

Franklin's deposition showcased his understanding of the guide's words. The darkened place was filled with the torment and disaster of many beings. It would house more as time drew onward. Franklin still pitied the beings there. Along with the sound of their misery, he felt guilty to be in such a place. He felt guilty spectating and reveling in his own solace knowing he wasn't in their predicament.

Franklin became dizzy. He indeed was distraught by everything he had seen. He was nearly fainting as several scenes spun in his mind. Starting to breathe in heavily, the foul air filled with the stench of sulfur began to fill his lungs to a degree near choking. He had to sit down on the path to catch his breath.

He placed his palms to his face and closed his eyes. He needed to try and gather himself as best he could. Franklin pulled his hands away, and he instantly became tense. Instead of being seated, he was now standing at the edge of another huge drop-off. His mouth fell open at what he saw. He was just seated, but if he had been nudged, he would have clearly fallen down a steep slope. Squeezing his eyes shut, he wished for it all to disappear somehow. It was an appalling spectacle. He opened his eyes to what appeared much closer than before.

Down below him was a beach full of thousands. They appeared to be waiting for something. That is when Franklin looked into the direction of where they were facing. It was out over the same sea from earlier that he saw the same rickety boat carrying some of them to the other side. The guide stood at the edge of the drop-off as well. He scanned over the beach down below as well.

Franklin's guide was wading in the tide of his old age. He was a wise, temperate, yet apathetic sort. He was surprisingly agile for his age though. Unlike Franklin, he felt no pity for the afflicted souls throughout the realm.

After an examination of the beachfront, the guide looked right down at the person Franklin was searching for. His high cheekbones were symmetrical as he gazed downward. His youthful sensibilities had all but faded. He was still slender despite his years, toned, and not at all stooped. Around his eyes were stress lines in just the right amount. At first his eyes were cast to the misty bedrock and then he turned to illustrate Franklin was right where he needed to be.

“What soon awaits those on the other side of the sea is for those who deliberately and consciously choose a way of life not consistent with love and purity of heart,” the guide said. “Consequently, there is also a place of reward for those who consciously choose a righteous way. Therefore, if there is a place across the sea for those who deliberately chose to do harm and chose to make wrong choices then there must be a place for those who chose the alternatives.

“Where you began here is the proper place for those who refused to make a choice. The uncommitted people of your world. Having been irresolute in life—that is, never making a choice for themselves—the uncommitted are stung constantly and provoked into movement. Among them are also those who have fallen due to their refusal to commit themselves to either side or the other. Their neutrality is their weakness.

“It is an understanding that in this place the uncommitted and the unwilling will now shed pieces of themselves unwillingly. No one here should be pitied. Remember—*the way in is the way out.*”

Awe transformed Franklin’s face as he allowed the guide’s words to resonate. His jaw tightened.

He responded, “I understand fully.”

"We will continue down toward the beach now," the guide declared. "We will take a different route."

The two walked away from the ledge and down a slope for quite some time until they arrived closer to the bottom. They stood before hordes of beings crowding the shore. They remained right at the edge of the long beach.

"What's happening here?" Franklin asked.

"This shore serves as the outer border of the *In Between*," the guide declared. "Until those here desire to make the crossing, then it is here where they will remain. But they are propelled to move by the demands of the ferryman, and divine poetic justice as well.

"Choosing to cross this sea is ultimately their final act of control. It is the point at which there will be no more indecision or otherwise. This beach is not merely just a foundation of small, rounded, rock crystals, and rounded detritus.

"No, this area serves as a precursor of things to come. Just as there was an appetite and choice for sin, vice, and the like on Earth then to leave this shore will be their choice as well. The way in is the way out."

At that very moment, Franklin observed the pandemonium ensuing on the crowded shoreline. On the beach were more males and females than he could ever count or imagine there being. It was clamor everywhere. Mayhem stood dead center in the middle of Franklin moving forward any further.

"Where do we go from here?" Franklin asked. "How do we get through this crowded beach? Didn't you say Danielle would be searching for the ferryman? If so, wouldn't she be here on this beach then?"

The guide took in the sight of the beach. His pupils flared as he peered out over the scene. Turning back towards Franklin he began to study him.

"This is the beach in which you will find Danielle," the guide affirmed. "The ferryman refuses to take anyone not of the dead across the sea. It is his strict endeavor to only take the dead across the sea. He will not accept you unless..."

"Unless what?" Franklin queried. "Unless what?"

"Unless you succumb in the real world," the guide replied. "If the soul no longer has responsibility in the real world, then..."

"But Dani was worse off you said," Franklin shouted. "That means she can die in our world and be stuck here! We have to find her now! If anyone gets on the boat then that means that they're dead, right? WE HAVE TO FIND HER NOW!!!

"I am sure you need to go no further than this beach Franklin," the guide confessed. "The one you seek is here among them."

The stench in the atmosphere smelled of burning and smoldering all over. It was pungent with the odor of decay and rot. Standing on the beach was more horrific than viewing it from afar. The sea still had the ailing creatures floating in it from before. There was no escape for them. Nothing but imminent damnation waited for those there. One by one more and more piled the shorefront from the opposite end.

Their piercing screams of trepidation continued to tear through Franklin's tranquility like paper mâché. His anxiety amplified to the tune of a battle drum as he'd become more desperate, terrified, and anxious.

In that instant, he began to remember lying to Dani during the week of the accident. He remembered being slew over the highway afterward like a low-end rag doll.

He could remember his mother's salty tears and the sprinkle of rain falling onto his cheek as he laid in the street of her neighborhood.

'*Who would comfort his family now?*' He thought.

He had walked down deeper into the crowd's eye before noticing it. The bumping and pushing of the crowd had quickly jousted him out of his brief daze. His guide was nowhere in sight.

Franklin was now caught in the middle of the frenzy. He could not see his guide with him anywhere. Looking in every direction, he could only see the thousands of despondent souls. He was trapped deep within the upheaval.

Chapter XXIX

Sometimes you have to lose your mind to find your freedom.

"DANIELLE, HONEY!! FRANKLIN BOOMED. "DANI!!!" His frantic screams were of no consequence. All of the commotion on the shore drowned out his shouting. Sounds of suffering and despair were at a higher pitch. He couldn't project louder than the crowd standing on the shorefront.

Franklin could see the ferryman coming back across the murky body of water. He wanted to outpace the ferryman at all costs. He had to find Dani, but the shore was too vast to cover alone. She could be anywhere.

The ferryman was the physical conduit used to lead every soul towards their last judgement. He steered them from the shore to the entry gates of the darkened place. The ferryman was also not hesitant by any means. He may have moved slow but his duties were never left undone. He was not prejudicial when it came down to using his huge wooden oar against procrastinators. Beings that covered the shore sometimes received echoing whacks from the long tool.

Franklin fought and clawed his way back out of the crowd from where he had entered. He sought after higher ground to try and locate his daughter quickly. Suddenly, he could feel a hand grabbing his arm. Fear overtook him. Some unknown hand had gripped his arm tightly. One of the beings was attempting to pull him back into the mass of chaos. Franklin began beating at the hand. The hand tugged away at him. It felt like the hand of a farmer or carpenter. Its power and rough callused grip was strong. Franklin had no recourse. He tried snatching away.

"LET GO OF ME!" Franklin demanded desperately.

He tried to yank away from the grip once more. Finally, he fell away from the crowd with another powerful thrust backward. Suddenly, the naked souls that stood around him begin to flee. An opening in the crowd revealed Franklin's guide standing nearby.

"Don't be afraid Franklin," his guide announced. "Why do you fear this place? You are but a stranger here. The way in is always the way out, yes?"

The middle-aged advisor climbed higher. He was back atop the summit where his guide was with little effort. He positioned himself at an angle to see what his guide saw. As he peered out over the beach he could see where Dani was in the distance.

"There she is Franklin," the guide professed. "She is

on the edge of the shore. She is waiting."

The beautiful young lady, months shy of adulthood, still had an aura that was hard to duplicate or suppress. Franklin's entire face lit up. In his mind the shore bank had become a beautiful tinted sepia, the sand was radiant, and the sea translucent. Franklin took in the sight of his daughter wholly. At that moment he saw no one but her. She was within the *In Between* with her father.

"Dani cannot see the world through my lens," he asserted. "It is a good thing that she cannot. She can still see possibilities that I cannot or would not at her age. All I saw was turmoil and a world of contention. My anger has led me to be one in the same with the very ones who have angered me.

"Imagine how alone and afraid she must be. She made it this far all on her own, and I put her in this predicament. But why should my darkness hold more peril for her than for myself?"

"I believe you will have the answer to that question sooner than you think Franklin," the guide replied. "Therefore, it is settled. This is where we depart from one another. Your daughter has been located and now it is up to you to choose wisely. It is up to you as it has always been.

"The ferryman will only take non-living souls across the borders to the other side. Living souls cannot pass. As long as her body holds up in the living world then she may not cross. Same as for you. The longer you are here then the more your soul seeks the land of the dead.

"Dani has been here for quite some time and her will to live will not hold much longer. Go to her, Franklin. I trust the choices you face ahead will be choices made of sound mind and judgement."

"I hope if I ever see you again that it is not in this place," Franklin said. "You don't belong here. Thank you for everything."

Franklin's emotions ran awry as he leaped down from the summit he stood upon. He sprinted along the beach edge. He did his best to bypass the occupants shuffling over the beach. He could see the ferryman's boat getting closer to the shore, but he focused in on Dani's position. He inhaled deeply before he let out a bellowing pronouncement.

"DANIELLE, STOP!" he cried out. "WAIT! STOP!"

On the other side of the beach Dani faintly heard Franklin's voice. Gazing in all directions, she could not capture where the sound was emanating from. Squaring her shoulders, she prepared herself for whatever the misty realm had to offer at the gates.

Then she could see a figure running toward her from several yards away. Franklin was beginning to come into view. At first, she was frightened by the charging figure. The star athlete did not know what it was.

The sound grew louder, but she still could not make out what it was she was hearing. Franklin's banter could be heard over the heavy commotion upon the shore. It was an incredible attempt at getting her attention.

"DANI!" Franklin continued. "DANI, IT'S DADDY! DANIELLE!!"

As Franklin drew closer, his voice grew louder. He frightened Danielle more than the beings surrounding them both. The ferryman was now less than a one hundred feet away from shore. Dani peered out toward the beckoning sound with half-lidded eyes. Recognition suddenly dawned upon her face. She could see it was a man. He was different than the rest of those on the shore bank.

"DANIELLE!!!" Franklin screamed with all of his might. "DANIELLE!!!"

Dani's face was overtaken by elation. She could finally hear him cogently.

"Dad?" she whispered.

Her face brightened as she repeated it again, "DAD!!"

Dani's face was no longer contorted by confusion. It was now lit up. She left from her spot on the shore and started running toward her name. Franklin kept screaming it loudly. He had found speed he didn't know he had as he ran nearer.

There they both were. Father and daughter caught in some forsaken place shut out from all they knew. Both father and daughter surveyed each other as they stopped a few feet short of an embrace.

They both needed to know if what they were seeing was authentic. They glared at each other intently. Could this be her father? Is it Franklin, the tall gentle giant Dani knew her father to be? Could it be Dani, the young lady Franklin had cradled in his arms when she was a child?

Dani's eyes became glossy as she glanced over at her father. Franklin was breathing quite heavily from his sprint. The effort of his run had begun to show, but it didn't matter to him. He had found his daughter. He had been through quite a lot to make it back to her, but it was worth the fight to see her face once more.

Chapter XXX

God has a plan, never lose hope.

DANI COULD NOT HIDE HER EMOTIONS AS her eyes welled over. Franklin approached her slowly and embraced her. They were reunited once again. All of the havoc and chaos surrounding them seemed to have stopped as they embraced. The wails and screams had become silent in that moment.

"Sorry, old man," Dani whispered. "I was looking for somewhere cold."

Her words barely parted her lips as she sobbed in Franklin's arms. Franklin held her close. He clenched her in his arms like a pitcher's mitt to a large hand. He too began to cry.

"I'm with you, Dani," he assured. "You got my full attention."

Franklin relaxed some. He had reunited with Danielle, but now they needed to escape the *In Between.* How, though?

"Dani, do you remember how you got here?" he asked. "How did you end up on this shore?"

"I don't remember how it all happened from start to finish," Dani answered. "All I remember is that there was silence. There was this feeling of nothingness. I can't really explain it, but I remember a calmness then a rush of energy.

"There was an extreme elation. It was a barrage of things happening inside of me. It sort of felt euphoric in a sense, but then I awoke here. I was alone. I wandered around an empty area for quite some time, but I couldn't hear or see anything. Then out of nowhere there was this pathway. I didn't feel the same but I also thought maybe I was among the dead since the last thing I remembered was the accident. So, I walked along the path, and it led me to someone."

"Who?" Franklin asked.

"He was a guide I believe," Dani replied. "He told me 'The way in was the way out'. He also said 'Change had to happen if release was desired.' Then he mentioned your name to me. He said I had to find you. So, that's what I set off to do. Nothing else mattered after that.

"He wouldn't tell me where you were specifically, but that you were here too. After he guided me over another area, I saw the Great Gates across the sea. I saw all the people in the waters too.

"The man told me that the longer I was here then the more the soul would desire to stay. I didn't care at that point. I had to find you! I had to. Nana, my scholarship, my friends, and even Mom couldn't have kept me from you. I love you, Dad!"

Franklin's eyes welled over. Tears fell in generous streams down his cheeks.

"Dani, I'm so sorry for not always being there," Franklin said. "I apologize for being more of a stranger than a father at times. I know my actions and deeds were not always the best, but something that doesn't deserve doubt is my love."

The two embraced deeply once more.

"You could've given up," Dani professed. "I could've given up. We both could've decided this place was too much, but we didn't. We made a choice to do whatever it took to find each other.

"We attract that which we are. The universe does not favor the greedy, the dishonest, nor the vicious; it helps the honest, the magnanimous, and the righteous."

"Who taught you that?" Franklin asked.

"Nana," Dani replied.

"She's a great teacher," Franklin acknowledged. "We'll see her again, but first we have to get off this beach."

At the exact same time, the ferryman had already made it ashore. He started loading his craft again. Franklin and Dani sprinted back toward the summit where Franklin entered the beach. It was the only exit Franklin was aware of. It was the way in. However, the shoreline was blocked by the ferryman and those departing with him.

"NEITHER OF YOU MAY PASS," shouted the ferryman. "Flee from this place! The living does not belong amongst the dead!"

"Which way is the way out?!" Franklin queried.

"The way out is the way in. Just as the way in is the way out," the ferryman replied.

The crowd behind them pushed further forward. The mood of the people swirled with sorrow and bitterness. Their attitudes resembled the attitude of the individual named William that Franklin had seen earlier. So many of them were begging for help beneath the surface.

However, some of them were accepting of whatever came next. They all stood frantic and nervous. They were facing their inevitable ends. Franklin and Dani inched themselves toward the easiest path away from the shorefront. They needed to get back near the mountainside. As they passed through the crowded shorefront, an individual fell out in front of their path. It was a female soul who was visibly weak and sickly. She winced when she began to speak.

"Help me!!" the woman pleaded. "You must help me! I don't belong here!"

Dani became frightened as the woman snatched at her feet. Instantaneously, a huge object swung past Dani and Franklin. It connected with the back of the woman's frame. Dani flinched at the impact.

The ferryman had taken his oar and struck the woman. By the looks of the wooden stick, it could be deduced that the ferryman used it often. There was no sympathy within the *In Between.* There were no boundaries. There was nothing but pain and sorrow.

"GET UP!" the ferryman commanded.

He grabbed the woman by the neck and flung her over near his decrepit boat. The capsule was an old master of the sea. The veteran planks preserved the odor of the souls even after all the brine splashed it over and over again.

The craft was sound despite its rickety frame. It was seaworthy enough to repeatedly take to the sea. It always appeared to be filled to its capacity each time Franklin had seen it. It also seemed to be a bit closer to capsizing each time due to its arrangement of occupants. It never did.

The ferryman, though senescent, was not as weak as he appeared. That was proved by every swing of his oar. He used it viciously across the backs and bodies of the laggards. He uttered a few words to Franklin and Dani before walking back to his boat.

He smirked at Franklin and urged, "Only the dead shall pass! No, one can run! No, one will be able to hide. No, one! Ever! Balance is inevitable! *Both* must balance."

Anxiety swelled deep in Franklin's gut. The ferryman's comments resonated deep with him. He remembered his conversation with *Both* and specifically what his guide kept saying. The way in is the way out.

"Dad?" Danielle questioned.

"Who else have you seen besides the guide Dani?" Franklin pressed.

"No, one." Dani declared. "What's happening now? What does he mean?"

"Don't worry," Franklin insisted. "I'll get us out of this. We have to keep moving. Stay close."

Finally, they made it back to the summit. The ledge was more than a rocky outcrop. The rocks had been formed by magma that cooled and then settled. It was all sediment from melted materials. The ledge was as wide as a single foot and maintained the same traction as a skating rink.

The path went right up the mountainside. Smooth dark granite against the metamorphic rock had to be billions of years old. Halfway up, Dani took a look back over the beach below. It remained filled with those who continued to wait for the ferryman to take them across. They almost resembled miniature figurines as Franklin and Dani climbed higher.

From her vantage point they could be easily hid behind her thumb. The screams could not be drowned out though. Yet, one wrong move and she would surely be back at the very bottom with them. It took effort to make it to the top of the sloped mountain.

Instantly, the ground began to quake. The heat from the surrounding atmosphere rose in temperature without warning. Dani and Franklin's ears rung with a new sound unfamiliar to them both. They dropped down to the mud beneath them. Dani slapped her hands over her ears as Franklin did the same.

He crawled over to Dani and clutched her underneath him. Across the sea beyond the Great Gates a blanket of lava flowed in thick rivers. The skies were now filled with more debris and a charcoal-colored mist. The magma's fiery coral glow lit up the darkness of the plain across from it.

Franklin grabbed Dani and lifted her off of the ground.

They froze for a moment where they stood to catch a glimpse across the sea. The illumination of the hot magma assisted in tracking the path. Both of them then ran without care. They were unaware of time and what might happen next.

Day and night had become blended as one in the *In Between.* Dani coughed and choked as the black heavy smoke covered the skies deep and wide. She managed to keep going. The smell of burning flesh and the dregs of what was left of the land filled the air again. Yet, they ran on as best they could across the barren plateau. They searched for any avenue of escape.

Chapter XXXI

Do what is right. Not what is easy.

AS FRANKLIN AND DANI CONTINUED ON, he thought of those he saw back on the beach. His emotions within the moment went back and forth from doubt to anxiety. Both Franklin and Dani were fatigued now. They slowed their pace down somewhere between a jog and a walk. They both peered out over the cliff at the dark sea below. The ferryman's boat pulled slowly across. For him, his task would never be complete. It would go on as it has forever.

'There couldn't be anyone down on the beach who didn't desire the light and warmth of the sun upon their face at least one more time.' He thought.

Nothing else really mattered or felt more important to the both of them than life now. Capturing missed opportunities, revitalizing relationships, and a chance for redemption pushed them.

"I want to wake up from this nightmare to the Georgia sun rising over the mountains," Dani admitted.

Before she could finish, the plain shifted again. This time it was not from the blast of hot magma. This time it was different, but not so much for Franklin. Franklin knew what was happening at that very moment. Rain from high above began to fall again. Beneath the sound of the pattering against her skin Dani could hear unintelligible sounds beginning to crescendo. She clutched tightly at her father's back.

Franklin could not see anything in any direction though. Suddenly, there he was. *Both* appeared out of thin air. He walked toward them slowly.

"Dani, stay close to me," Franklin ordered.

Both wasn't the biggest or scariest figure Franklin had seen since he'd arrived, but he was terrifying nonetheless. *Both* had a voice that wielded all in the *In Between.* Then as surely as Franklin assumed it would, the surrounding area began to transpose. Only this time it was into a dark four walled room of all black.

At that same moment *Both* placed Dani inside an alternate reality also. She was able to see Franklin's idle body inside his hospital room. Machines whistled around him as he lay without movement.

The walls of the room Franklin were a part of blocked out all sound and rumblings. He investigated the dimension of the room. He no longer felt Dani grabbing onto him. He had been separated from her with little knowledge of it. As expected, the room transposed once more. This time, Franklin was placed back into the offices of Mitchell, Leonard, and Maxwell. He could see before him a vision of Jacob Jr. and his father Jacob Sr. Both men reveled the demise of Arthur Mitchell.

"Finally, the old man decided to sprout his wings," Junior mocked. "I thought when old Lenny left the firm that Arthur surely wouldn't take this long to follow him into retirement. Death had to finally take him out. It was no quit in that bastard that's for sure. Remember Lenny said something to you the day we forced him out? Do you remember what he said?"

"Keep your voice down son," Jacob Sr. responded. "If I remember correctly, the old bastard said to me, 'Be careful who you choose to call your friends. You're better off having four quarters than one hundred pennies. I remember smiling at him when he said it. He said that to me on his last day as a matter of fact.

"To his credit he was one of the original '*Mad*' men like your grandfather. Although, it's true what he said, Arthur should have been the man he mentioned it to. With Arthur out of the picture we can proceed with taking back what's rightfully ours. He should have never taken my father's company. It should have been mine, but today I'm one more step closer to procuring it back."

The father and son tandem smiled at one another with broad grins. Arthur's death, though sudden, was an opportune time to procure back a business rooted deeply in the Maxwell name.

"Pop, you know we still have quite a bit of work to finish though," Junior advised. "We still need majority vote to get Denise out. Then it's done and official. That's not going to be an easy feat, though.

"I mean Arthur is gone for sure, but what about Franklin? He's still around."

"From the looks of his injuries he may not be for much longer," Mr. Maxwell asserted.

"I hope you're right," Junior replied. "So, what if Denise gets a great deal of support from the board? She is a grieving widow, you know?"

"Don't worry, son," Mr. Maxwell responded. "Don't worry. The lure has been cast."

"Awesome!" Junior gloated. "Now the company can be back in the hands that it belongs in."

Within the *In Between,* Franklin became enraged at the sight of the Maxwell family's plots and schemes.

"WHY ARE YOU SHOWING ME THIS?!!" Franklin exploded.

The middle-aged advisor's temper had boiled over. Both spectacles inside the rooms were so authentically real. Then as quickly as they appeared, they were transformed again. Dani and Franklin were now back on top of the pathway from before.

"Dad, are you okay?" Dani asked.

Franklin gestured with a thumb.

"What does sacrifice mean to you Franklin?" *Both* asked aloud. "Your way out is your way in. You always have a choice, but will it be reprisal or self-sacrifice? Circumstance certainly is not at all happenstance. It was by your own choice you have set in motion a series of events that led you here. Nothing is by default Franklin."

"Why, now?" Franklin asked.

"No one is exempt from the aftermath of cause," *Both* mentioned. "The forces transmigrating over time whether short or long will abridge nonetheless."

"I realize now for the very first time that there are much bigger things than myself and my trivial endeavors," Franklin confessed. "Although I have seen many places and horrors in my time, none come close to anything like this.

"I have seen the monumental agony and despair on the many faces holding residency in this dark place. I have seen the brutality of its very existence weigh heavy on the doubtful here. However, had it not been for choice then the recipients of this dreadful place would not be subjected to all it has to offer.

"I recognize that this place is only for one's who choose it. It is for individuals that are not strangers to darkness. This place cannot harbor the righteous and pure at heart. What does sacrifice mean to me you ask? It's simple. It means giving up something, but not giving up on something. It means losing much to gain so much more."

Franklin glanced over at his daughter and held his next words briefly. He stared deep into her hazel eyes. Sadness clouded his features. Over the next few seconds, he remembered her childhood. Her first steps and first words replayed in his mind.

Dani loomed toward her father and embraced him tightly. He fit snug in her arms as a Joey in its mother's pouch. His expression hardened. He turned to face *Both.*

"Have the sins of the father befallen on the son?" he asked rhetorically. "Do I want my father's enemies to account for what they have done? Maybe the old me would think selfishly and beg for revenge, but what does it matter now. So, one sows shall one reaps."

Franklin turned to look into Dani's hazel eyes once more. There was a rawness to her expression. There was a sadness that hovered over them both. She made no attempt to conceal or even wipe away her own tears as they rolled down her cheeks.

"It's a test," Franklin stated. "Choice could put us here, but only if we choose irresponsibly. You don't belong here, and you wouldn't be here if it weren't for my ways. You should be with your friends and your mother. I keep being told 'The way in is the way out'. I believe I know what it means now. I made a promise I would never leave you again. No, matter what, and I easily decided upon that.

"It is by the choices we make that create our own happiness or despair. It is by choice alone that we craft our very circumstance, and here we are. It's me who has been so filled with so much rage to become greater than your Pawpaw that I lost sight of things more important than my own spiteful ambitions.

"Being a father to you. Just being their period. My selfishness and desire to hurt the ones who have hurt me led me to this. My lack of understanding and lack of forgiveness has strained relationships worthy of fixing.

"On the inside there was nothing. I was hollow and numb. I did not consider how my thoughts and ideas could affect you, or anyone else around me in the ways that they have. I've seen various troubles in my search for you. An individual's current state depicts past actions that then create an everlasting future. I understand it now.

"You're only here because of a choice you were about to make in trying to find me. However, even by making that choice would be against the great law forbidding suicide.

You were choosing to let go of your worldly life in search of me if it meant it. But that sacrifice I believe is what has kept you alive. Your strength and willingness to fight until the task is done. Your willingness to sacrifice your own self-interests. Who says a daughter can't teach her father?

"I can only hope I have earned your trust now. I never strayed, betrayed, or abandoned you because of who you are. It has only been because of who I am. I haven't always been stalwart, true, and loving I know now. But to keep you safe I am willing to do whatever it takes.

"I don't ever want you to feel bitter, angry, and upset because of all the times I've lied. My heart still beats for you and your mother back in that hospital room.

"You still have time and much more in store to grow. Improvement and growth are necessary, but as for me it may be too late. So how do I choose? Do, I choose to maintain my selfishness to get back at the Maxwell family, or do I accept the choices I've made thus far?"

Franklin juggled his next words carefully.

He simpered in suspense as he answered himself, "I'm sorry Dani, but it looks like I won't be keeping my promise to never leave you alone again."

Chapter XXXII

Happiness is a choice, not a result.

"MY LIFE FOR MY DAUGHTER'S LIFE IS not something I could never hesitate in trading," Franklin fervently announced. "To remain here in this place will be my burden and mine alone."

"NO!" Dani shouted. "DAD!! D—"

Before Dani could finish her sentence, the atmosphere rapidly transformed. She gripped Franklin as tight as she could, but Franklin vanished within her grasp. Nothing remained but Dani and *Both.*

Dani's body shook. Fret filled her stomach cavity as she was left feeling empty. Dani cried out into the skies only to be drowned out by the other sounds and wails. The moans and screams could be heard once again at a deafening pitch.

"What have you done to my father?" Dani griped.

"It is so. The free will of man is not directed by either I or anything else but himself," Both explained. "I do not find pleasure or feel any attachment to the decisions of man. It is only I which presents in the conscious mind opportunity or thereby a possibility. Therefore, I am an eventuality. I am an eventuality that you have complete power over to control.

"You like your father and many more before and after him will always have the power to choose your own fortune. Whether it doom or arcadia I have no proxy in the matter. Only you decide which is chosen between the parallel routes you create.

"So, what happens next?" Danielle asked. "What do I do now?"

"I'll let you decide," *Both* replied.

Both disappeared from sight. Franklin's choice had been made. Dani fell backward onto her back. As she tried to make sense of what happened, she dematerialized where she laid. The *In Between* was a distant memory now. It was over.

Chapter XXXIII

You never know how strong you are until

being strong is the only choice you have.

MEANWHILE, INSIDE OF DANI'S HOSPITAL room, Vivienne sat alone quietly. As the days came and went, she'd lost herself in the situation. It was more than a surreal feeling. It was much more like a bad dream she could not forget. It was within those hospital walls that she knew she could not escape the buildup of a climactic end. Anxiousness coursed through her body daily. She could not shake her grief. She tried night in and night out, but most often she did not succeed.

She worried constantly. There were things she felt she should have done on the night of the accident but didn't. Coupled with her own self-criticism, Vivienne's last text to her husband stood out and dominated her mind. She thought about her actions and words. She found them abrasive and a bit overboard.

Festering guilt rendered her mind helpless, but all Vivienne could do was wait as her impatience and anxiety continued to reach peak levels. Shortly, Doctor Hills would be by to check on Dani. Up to that point he had been very helpful and forthcoming. In any other clothes he would appear too young for the job though. If seen in cargo shorts and a V-neck t-shirt he could pass as a freshman in college.

He had a face like the neighborhood milkman or someone you'd ask for directions in the street. He was very neighborly and open. He also paid close attention to the opinions of the hospital nurses and what they had to say. He spoke without the jargon Vivienne feared most doctors were guilty of.

"Good morning, Mrs. Mitchell," Doctor Hills asked. "How are we feeling today?"

"I'm fine, doctor," Vivienne mustered out. "How are you?"

"Under the circumstances I am well," he replied. "Thank you, for asking."

He paused at speaking after his greeting to check Dani's chart at the end of her bed. He visibly relaxed and broke into a slight smile. For the most part Vivienne understood what was going on and periodically Doctor Hills would stop to address her and the next steps.

It was comforting. He never made Vivienne not feel Dani's well-being was most important. It was though all she had to do was say "no more" and Doctor Hills would listen. But Vivienne would never say that. No matter how hopeless she was. She always had an inkling of faith through her sadness. Even though it was a traumatic situation, she held on as best she could.

"Danielle is still stable and has functional brain activity," Doctor Hills began. "We will continue to monitor and test her further. There is still a reasonable chance she can make it through this and live a healthy productive life."

Vivienne sighed. She propped her chin on her hand before she responded, "Thank you, doctor. Thank you."

Dani laid in her bed quietly. Her breath matched the beeping of the machines positioned next to her. The sounds were the only indications of her heartbeat. The only indications of her existence.

"Doctor, I can't heal her," Vivienne remarked. "I've been sitting here day in and day out thinking of ways how I could help her in some way.

"It is in these times you begin to look at life differently. You form a different perspective. You learn that life is much more precious than you ever thought possible. You learn that your very own quiet place is all you have left.

"That scampering mind of yours is looking for solutions, a way to fight for life and live meaningfully—to thrive. Our minds are more powerful than we showcase and our hearts way stronger than we share. However, the quieter I become, the harder it becomes for me. The deeper my love grows for my husband and daughter.

"I've been watching and listening to their heartbeats. You know, sometimes the best conversations are the ones when you don't speak. My husband and I have had plenty over the last day or so. Both of them are whispering to me doctor. 'Mom it will be okay' 'Vivienne, I love you'. The longer I sit in my own quiet place then the more I find out about them. The more I find out about myself. I just want them back, doctor. I need them back."

"Mrs. Mitchell, I will do everything in my power to get them back to you," the doctor encouraged. "I am extremely humbled you are willing to share as much as you have with me. I will only ask that you stay strong for yourself and for them as well. I will check back in a little while."

"Thank you, doctor," Vivienne added.

The doctor checked Dani's vitals once more then he exited the room. Once again it was just Dani, Vivienne, and her thoughts.

Although it was still morning, Vivienne dozed off to sleep. Shortly, thereafter a slight sound danced lightly across the hospital room. It made enough of a fuss to alert Vivienne's senses. Her eyes lazily rolled open. They were glazed over with remnants of a dream she was having. Then the sound intensified.

Vivienne was awakening to see the ECG stimulated by a higher rate of activity than what it had been. She yawned long and wide from still being half asleep. She crept closer to the monitor.

'*Could she be dreaming*?' She thought.

The beeping continued to grow. Then she noticed movement from the bed. She peered away from the electrocardiogram, and then over to Danielle's left hand. Out of the corner of her eye she thought she'd seen it move.

Vivienne covered her mouth with both hands. She did not want it to be a false alarm if she screamed out. Her leg muscles tightened as she stood beside her child. The hair on her arms and neck bristled from the shock of what she was witnessing. However, she needed more.

"Come on, Danielle," she whispered. "Come on, baby. Show me again. Wake up!"

Vivienne started towards the room exit. The monitor continued to intensify with steady beeps. Vivienne almost fell backward over her chair as she inched closer to the door. She never turned her sight away from her child. Suddenly, Danielle gave her the sign she had been waiting on for days. Danielle's entire hand shuddered.

Vivienne ran out of the room yelling, "Nurse!!"

A nurse met her halfway down the corridor before they raced back into Dani's room. Doctor Hills and a few other scrub wearing clinicians arrived shortly thereafter. Dani's room was now a spectacle to behold.

As the sun crept from behind the skyline of the city, Vivienne felt more optimistic than ever before. Although Dani did not regain complete consciousness right at that time, it wasn't foolhardy to think she was going to pull through this.

It was now a question of how long would it be before she did. The hour drew late, and all the nurses had long since left the room. However, Dani was still being closely monitored. Every hour, without fail, the vital checks were completed.

It was up to Dani now. She just needed to break through. Danielle was a fighter. It was just a matter of timing. Vivienne, of course, was extremely anxious for any new updates. She waited and she watched Dani carefully for any sudden movements. Wide-eyed and restless, she couldn't even imagine being asleep at a moment like that.

A few more hours had passed before Vivienne's eyes began to drift though. It was three a.m. and she could feel herself slowly beginning to doze off. As her head lolled down into her bosom, her eyelids were closed trunk tight. Her breath was even and calm. The expression on her face was no longer of zeal but relaxation.

Before she could float deeper into the REM levels of her much-needed slumber, she was teased by a faint sound. It was a familiar sound. There it was again. It tickled her ears, and it made Vivienne flinch in her sleep. But the sound was still too low and incoherent to wake her. Then it grew louder. Finally, Vivienne's sleep was broken. Denise had come by in the middle of the night and fell asleep next to her. She was seemingly too tired to have been woken up by the faint actions.

Her oval shaped face scrunched up. Her lashes fluttered faster than Hummingbird wings. Her awareness was opening up to what was happening., Vivienne heard the noise again. This time she heard it clearer.

"Dad," a voice whispered.

Chapter XXXIV

Not all storms come to disrupt your life,

some come to clear your path.

"DENISE, WAKE UP HONEY," VIVIENNE BURSTED out. "Denise, wake up!"

Denise woke up confused and disheveled from Viviene's antics.

"I'm awake," Denise confirmed. "I'm awake. What's wrong?"

"It's Danielle," she admitted.

Denise jolted up from her chair. She wiped her eyes with the palms of her hands.

"What about Danielle?" Denise asked.

Then the softest, calmest, and most angelic sound whispered to them both. It was a sound they hadn't heard in such a long time.

"Mom," Dani mumbled. "Mom?"

Vivienne froze where she stood. She couldn't move. It felt as though she had weights wrapped around her ankles. Both women's eyes were wide enough to show all the white.

"Danielle?" Vivienne muttered.

Vivienne clutched her chest. Denise rushed over to see if what she thought she heard was accurate. She brushed her hand through Dani's hair. Could Dani really be out of her coma? Denise's inclination was confirmed.

"Vivienne, I'll go get some help," she said.

Denise scurried out of the room for help quickly, but to Vivienne everything seemed to be moving in slow motion. She stepped over to Dani's bedside. Dani's eyes darted underneath her eyelids as she tried desperately to open them. Left then the right eyelid opened. Vivienne gasped at the sight. It moved her to tears immediately.

"My, baby," she rejoiced. "Oh, my baby."

Everything was blurry to Dani at first. She didn't know where she was, or how she'd gotten in her hospital bed. Things would slowly take time to process. The flat surface high above her was the ceiling. The shadowy figure standing over her was her mother. The beeping she heard was her own heartbeat. Very slowly and gradually, Dani's cognition started to return.

Doctor Hills arrived with a slew of clinicians to examine her. He wanted to check her verbal and voluntary responses to command.

"Okay, we need to get her down and prepped for an MRI and CT scan," the doctor announced. "Mrs. Mitchell, we are going to run a few tests on Danielle, okay? We want to take a look at her brain activity and cognition. Everyone let's go. Danielle, can you hear me?"

"Yes," Danielle said softly.

Denise raced down the hall to Franklin's room. What she saw once she opened the door made her stop right in her tracks. It was Daniel. He was standing over Franklin's bedside. He didn't even turn his head to face Denise as she entered.

"Get away from my son!" she demanded. "DANIEL, I SAID GET AWAY FROM HIM!"

"Most times the right thing to do isn't the easiest thing to do," Daniel said. "But it seems the right thing for your son wasn't difficult at all."

Denise shut her eyes tight. She whispered a prayer to herself before reopening the windows to her soul. She noticed Daniel had vanished. Within a matter of seconds, he was gone.

To Denise's amazement, Franklin's ECG monitor increased in tempo. A nurse arrived to Franklin's room at the same time of the occurrence. She noticed the machine's activity and ran away for assistance. Denise did not move an inch. Joy overtook her features instantly. Her eyes glossed over from a flood of tears.

Franklin slightly lifted his head from the bed, and spoke to his mother for the first time in a great while, "Dad told me to tell you, 'He loves you'.

Chapter XXXV

There will be hard days, but they won't last.

A FEW WEEKS OR SO HAD PASSED BEFORE Danielle and Franklin were both able to leave the hospital. They had been fortunate enough to regain full mobility and cognition. Both were recovering well enough to speak and remember events from their lives prior to the accident. Gradually, they both remembered the wreck, but they could not remember much of anything pertaining to the events leading up to it.

"Son, how are you feeling," Mrs. Mitchell asked.

Franklin took in a sharp breath that pained him before he responded, "I'm fine, I guess. In ways I don't know how

I feel. I'm exhausted, and I feel like I've ran ten marathons. With more therapy, physically my body will get there I suppose. Mentally and emotionally I just don't know yet. It'll take time."

A sad smile shown on Mrs. Mitchell's face.

"As soon as you are able to, I want you to visit Arthur with me. Just the two of us. You know your father could be very ambitious, but he was a great man. He was a really great husband. He was always doing the best he could.

"He was always looking out for his family. Even in death he did the necessary things to make sure we wouldn't be left out to dry. He was everything I could've asked for in a husband."

The cords stood out in Franklin's neck. He placed his hands onto his mother's. She was still wearing her wedding ring from so many seasons ago. He gazed into her eyes.

As he began to speak, his voice cracked, "He knows mother, and I know."

Mrs. Mitchell embraced her son. Franklin's mind swam with the thoughts of his father, but also with the thoughts of his daughter.

Suddenly, the hospital room door opened. It was Vivienne, one of the hospital nurses, and Dani. Dani strolled inside in a wheelchair. She was still weak and awfully fatigued. Dani was capable of getting around, but it was more precautionary to use the aid of the chair apparatus during that time. The corners of Franklin's mouth quirked up.

"Hey, you!!" Franklin quipped.

"HEY, OLD MAN!!" Dani replied.

Their feelings may not have always been shown, but it was different now. In that moment, Dani sat there staring at her father as he stared back. Faced with a question of sacrifice in the most grotesque, hideous, and horrendous place, he chose to sacrifice his own life for hers.

She thought she had lost him again. He chose something over his own vices. He chose her over getting revenge. He *chose* her. Dani's chin trembled as she took in the sight of her father.

A broad smile covered Dani's cheerful face. She stood up from the chair on wheels, and flung herself onto her father.

"Thanks for not breaking your promise, old man," Dani whispered. "Find you in a cold place, huh?"

"Well, I must say, Franklin Terry Mitchell, you have had everyone on a real scare this past month," Vivienne started.

Vivienne rested her hands on her hips as she geared up for a speech. Her eyebrows pointed inward.

"Vivienne, let the boy be," Denise ordered.

"Mother, I want to say this," Vivienne contended firmly. "These feelings I have will not and have not ended for your son. The day they do will be the day my body ceases to function here on this earth. I hope that our love always endures.

"I have been given more blessings than I feel worthy of, Franklin. I still feel love, joy, and happiness so strongly with you that it gives me chills right down in the center of my being.

"However, I've known pain with you. I've known so much that you would think I'd be immune to it by now.

Pain I've never really spoken on, but pain I believe has and will help you and I understand each other better. Pain that I feel has been necessary for our growth. Pain I wouldn't want to feel or go through with anyone else."

Franklin's features suspended between overwhelming joy and humility. Vivienne face palmed. Her eyes were now red as the sash of Captain Kidd as she tried wiping away salty streams from her cheeks. She walked over to the opposite side of his bed, and laid her head down across his chest. She could hear his heartbeat

The warmth of his body met hers. One of his hands clasped around her lower back as his other hand stroked her hair. With each touch more tears fell. After so many years together, Franklin knew there was nothing more he needed or wanted.

The things he had been trying so hard to accomplish weren't important now. Not money, not fame, or the recognition. All he wanted was his family. All he wanted was time to make new memories and better choices. Wasting that wasn't something he had on his agenda.

"Well, I must say that this has been a glorious day," Mrs. Mitchell declared. "I also want to say that I love all three of you very deeply. So did Arthur. I have my granddaughter back with her father and a daughter-in-law back with the family she loves.

"LORD, WHAT A DAY!! I don't want to rush away, but if you all will excuse me, I have business to attend to today."

"Okay, mother," Franklin replied. "Do what's best. Just try not to hurt any of those snakes too bad."

With a face-wide smile and her head held high, the matriarch responded the only way she knew how, “I won’t make any promises.”

Chapter XXXVI

Move in silence, Only speak when it's time to say CHECKMATE!

IT TOOK DENISE A HALF HOUR TO GET TO the firm's office tower. Her disposition exuded calmness as she rode up the elevator to the emergency board meeting. It was her time to showcase her wits and everything Arthur had taught her. In life, he depended on her. In his death, she saw it no different.

The elevator chimed as it arrived on the boardroom floor. At first glance it appeared everyone had already arrived. They were still fraternizing amongst themselves. Real ink couldn't have written purpose on Mrs. Mitchell's face greater. A plump, brassy, extremely well-to-do brunette named Carol C. Crawford, made her way toward Mrs. Mitchell.

"Hello, Denise," Carol started. "What a day isn't it? It's just glorious outside. Thanksgiving will soon be here, and there is so much to be thankful for don't you agree? The sun is shining, and here we are still witnessing its beautiful glory."

"Carol, I will have to say you're right," Mrs. Mitchell responded. "It is a glorious day. A glorious day indeed! Excuse me."

Mrs. Mitchell walked away from Mrs. Crawford toward her seat. Maxwell Sr. stepped into her path before she could make it there. He forced a smile on his face.

"How are you, Denise?" he asked. "I do apologize we have not had the opportunity to speak in full since Arthur's passing. However, I just want you to know that I will be sure to take care of this firm as if it were Arthur himself still at the helm."

"Well, I appreciate that very much so, Jacob," Mrs. Mitchell acknowledged. "I'm sure you will do just that if given the opportunity."

"I'd like to call to order the Mitchell, Leonard, and Maxwell board of directors meeting," John Fong, the meeting chair, announced. "I'd also like to do a roll call. I, John Fong, am present. Carol Crawford, Barbara Becker, Robert Bishop, William Buck, Audra Densford, Tommie Emerson, Denise Mitchell, Evelyn Ruggerio, Junior Maxwell Sr., Anji Todd, and Nathaniel Woods are all present. We do have a quorum. Are there any late additions to the agenda? All those in favor of today's agenda say I."

Everyone in the meeting replied, "I."

"It's unanimous," John announced. "Do I have any motions to approve the agenda?"

Finally, after much of the "Robert's Rules of Order" finished, items of old business were started and discussed completely. New business was to be addressed thereafter. A motion was made and seconded in regards to the next items. Leadership moving forward for the firm was to be discussed.

"Let me start off by saying good morning, friends and colleagues," Maxwell Sr. boomed from the front of the room. "What a day like today for new beginnings. A marvelous day it is! Unfortunately, this will be our first meeting without our beloved Arthur Mitchell. It is still such an incredible loss and tragedy to our great firm. Our hearts continue to go out to his lovely wife and the family.

"But now it is understood by this board that his share of business, assets, and interests have been passed on to his Mrs. Denise. However, with Arthur's recent death comes a succession scenario we must address.

"Since his passing, it means that Mrs. Mitchell is now an acting general partner alongside Gordon Woods Capital Partners, Nathaniel Wood's Hedge Fund, and myself, I believe based on our existing partnership agreement and its clauses there is an obligation for her to sell her stake in the general partnership.

"Now if I am not mistaken it is binding. But there's no way possible for me to believe that Mrs. Mitchell is even capable of continuing in her husband's seat. Not as the face and leader of this firm. I motion to dismiss her as the acting chair. Effect—"

"Ease off of your engine just one minute there Little Red Corvette," Denise interjected.

"Excuse me?" Jacob barked. "What did you just say?"

"I believe you heard me," Denise replied. "Now I understand that I am not my husband. No one in this room *is* as a matter of fact. Not any of us! Especially, not you Mr. *Corvette.*

"I did not ask for this role or position. That much is true. Now I have thought about this long and hard, but I couldn't bring myself to a decision on what to do. So, I asked myself, 'What more could I do if I did not want the position?' I came up with a solution. I will agree to a buyout."

The room's occupants gasped at her words. Commotion filled the boardroom like the Georgia sun behind them. Jacob could not help hiding his pleasure with Denise's offer. A mocking smile covered his face.

"However, there is one thing I would like to add before we get the particulars out of the way," Denise emphasized. "While I was pondering what to do after Arthur's passing, I received a call from a very special friend. A dear friend to the Mitchell family in fact.

"All of you would be surprised by what I was told. Oddly enough I can't say that I was quite truthfully. After the call and the conversation, I was prompted to call another friend that is seated at this very table. I gave him an offer also.

"He has always known just as I have known that a wolf is still a wolf no matter how well it dresses. I would like it to be known that there has been a conflict of interest among our partners. A conflict of interest that not only supersedes any buyout discussion, but also calls for an immediate termination or resignation of those conflicting the interests."

"A CONFLICT OF INTEREST?" Jacob poked. "Denise, cut the antics! It's over! Arthur is gone and you're out! Now can we proceed with my motion please?!"

"I don't understand, Mrs. Mitchell," John Fong said. "Where is all of this going? What did you find out and about whom?"

"Well, it must be stated that someone in this room has been under federal investigation for quite some time now," Denise replied. "If you will allow me to introduce another one of my friends."

Denise walked away from the boardroom table and toward the door. She opened it revealing a man in his mid-forties dressed in a navy-blue business suit.

"Before Arthur died, he was contacted by my friend here, Mr. Collin Newman, an Assistant United States Attorney, about the dealings of a one Mr. Raymond Algieri for reasons I cannot disclose.

"As you all know the Maxwell family closed a multi-million-dollar deal with Algieri's IPSOS Corporation. However, what you did not know is—well, I'll let Mr. Newman continue. Mr. Newman, will you please?"

"Good morning, ladies and gentleman. I apologize for the intrusion. However, Mr. Raymond Algieri is currently being indicted on conspiracy to money laundering, straw picking, and violation of the RICO act," Mr. Newman started. "It is our understanding that one, Mr. Jacob Maxwell has had a long upstanding relationship with Mr. Algieri for quite some time, along with another man we cannot disclose. This relationship dates back more than a decade, and Mr. Maxwell has allegedly assisted in these dealings. The intention was quite clear."

"YOU DIRTY FILTHY BASTARD!" Tommie Emerson yelled. "You've been laundering money in our firm? I knew never to trust you and your silver tongue proclamations!"

"Special Agent Newman, sir, for how long?" Carol Crawford asked.

"Well, ma'am it seems for quite some time," Mr. Newman responded. "This is a federal indictment I hold here, Mr. Maxwell. Mr. Jacob Maxwell Jr. has already been taken into custody under conspiracy to money launder as well."

"Well, I believe that constitutes as a conflict of interest wouldn't you say Jacob?" Denise challenged.

Other federal agents entered into the boardroom to assist Special Agent Newman.

"Mr. Jacob Foley Maxwell, you are under arrest for the conspiracy to commit money laundering and securities fraud," Mr. Newman explained.

"No, arrest who?" Jacob clamored. "This is beyond ludicrous. I'm not going anywhere with anyone. I haven't done anything!"

All of Jacob's attention beamed into Denise's direction.

"I have to admit something to you Denise, I think I may have underestimated you. My lawyer is going to have all of your asses for this! Watch and see!

"But there is one thing I think you should be aware of. I may have underestimated you, Denise, but by all means don't UNDERESTIMATE ME!"

He smashed his fist on the wood table. He then chuckled softly.

"Soon and I mean very soon I'll see you again. This isn't over! It's far from over! Your husband never deserved my father's company! Tell Leonard Gordon he didn't deserve it either! My father ruined us when he sold out to your lousy husband.

"At least Leonard knew when to just leave. Why couldn't Arthur just leave?! After all I've done for this company, there was no way I could've ever let your gutless waste of a son *supersede me*! He could never lead this firm!

Jacob's voice broke as the agents apprehended him.

"This is not the end of what my family is!" Mr. Maxwell continued. "THIS IS NOT THE END FOR US!"

The agents had begun to lead him out of the boardroom. Suddenly, Nathaniel Woods walked toward Mr. Maxwell. Nathaniel, a leading partner in the firm, had a rigid expression embossed on his face. He tried his best to speak through his pursed lips.

"Jacob, my father wanted me to share something with you," he said.

"Your father?" Jacob asked. "Who's your father? I don't even know your father!"

"Before it's said by anyone else, I wish to tell you something," Nathaniel started. "I'd like to relay something to you because it's important that you know. My father thought it apropos to mention his favorite saying under these circumstances. He told me to say 'Be careful who you choose to call your friends. A man is better off having a few solid quarters than many pennies."

Jacob's face went white. The muscles in his face pulled his eyebrows together in a frown. His eyes darted around the room. His sheer shock of the quote wouldn't allow him to focus on one thing.

"I don't understand," Mr. Maxwell said. "Your father told you that?! Lenny? Lenny is your father?"

"He did and yes, he is," Nathaniel answered. "My father and your former partner, Leonard Gordon, told me to remind you because it seems you may have forgotten. I think by now you are intelligent enough to deduce who will be buying Mrs. Mitchell out. Which will still keep a Mitchell at the top. His first name is Franklin."

Jacob remained quiet. He was shocked by the comments Nathaniel made. His nostrils flared from his rage.

"Apologies for not mentioning it sooner," Denise interrupted. "The man before you is Nathaniel Woods, but he was born Nathaniel Gordon. The heir of *the* Mr. Leonard Gordon. You ruined your big surprise, Jacob! Who knew this would be the day you took your leave?!"

"Jacob it's true," Nathaniel declared. "I must honestly say from the moment we met I never trusted you. So, imagine how we felt when Special Agent Newman contacted us and Mrs. Mitchell about his federal investigation into your nefarious practices.

"Since we're all being Frank, no pun intended, Arthur always had something every great leader had. He had ethics, and that is something you just don't possess Jacob. In my eyes you are nothing short of an embarrassment to the Maxwell name.

"If there was anything my father taught me, it was always having contingencies. There is no way you could've thought you'd ever be at the helm of this firm or be a partner of my fund. EVER! Now if you'll excuse us, we all have work to do."

On cue, the federal agents along with Special Agent Newman walked Jacob out of the office into the hallway. He directed the agents to continue searching the Maxwell offices since a warrant had already been signed.

"Daniels, perfect timing," Special Agent Newman remarked. "Mr. Maxwell, say hello to your escort downstairs. This is Special Agent Daniels. He's rather new to the crew, but you'll be in safe hands with him.

"Daniels, take Mr. Maxwell down for transport. Also see that agents Mahoney and Griggs assist you in the lobby. I'll be down in just a moment."

Agent Daniels led the handcuffed Mr. Maxwell onto the nearest elevator. The doors closed quicker than Mr. Maxwell was accustomed to. The lights inside of the lift flickered brightly. He scanned the four walls of metal box.

The lights continued to shimmer in the elevator much brighter and much hotter. Special Agent Daniels never broke his burning gaze over Mr. Maxwell the entire time. He stepped closer toward him and clasped his hands on both his shoulders. The gesture took Mr. Maxwell by surprise.

"Can I ask you something?" Agent Daniels asked. "What would you do to get your father's firm back?"

☞

Back in the boardroom Denise had continued, "Although, Jacob has successfully ruined his reputation, John and I think we missed a vote on his motion."

"Due to the extreme nature of this situation, I think it may prove most prudent to postpone the vote," John stated. "For now, Mrs. Denise Mitchell is chair of Mitchell, Leonard, and Maxwell Partners."

"I agree," Denise charged. "However, I would like to motion for a dissolution of the current partnership with Mr. Jacob F. Maxwell Sr. effective immediately pending his criminal investigation into money laundering and securities fraud. This is in accordance to our company bylaws. We will also need to prepare for SEC and FINRA inquests into his dealings."

"I'll have to bring in the litigation team," John replied. "This fallout will need very meticulous PR to fix this mayhem. No one speaks to the press. We will need all resources on this."

"We'll see it done," Denise encouraged. "Nathaniel and I will move to continue under a newly formed partnership with a newly appointed CEO. I think we are in agreement on a very special someone."

Denise gave Nathaniel a warming smile.

"Okay, ladies and gentlemen. We will adjourn this board meeting until further notice." John advised.

As the meeting cleared out into the corridor, there were agents moving everywhere. There was a high percentage of them in both of the Maxwell offices. Mrs. Mitchell called for the elevator. It arrived in no time. She stepped inside and glanced up at one of the television sets. She caught a glimpse of the latest newscast. It showed a special report that read:

Breaking News - Mr. Raymond Algieri, the IPSOS corporation founder, has been taken into custody at his home by federal agents.

Denise arrived on the twenty-third floor with thoughts and fond memories of Arthur on her mind. She exited the elevator and walked over to the biggest window on the floor. Down below she could see several media outlets beginning to swarm the parking lot. A gentle smile illuminated her face.

She gazed out into the afternoon sun, and celebrated softly to herself, 'What a day, Lord! Lord, what a day!'

Epilogue

A little over a year passed before both Franklin and Dani fully recovered from their accident. Unsurprisingly, there wasn't any timetable that was set for the emotional recovery of the events they witnessed in the *In Between.*

Nonetheless, it significantly changed the entire family for the better. Dani is currently in her first semester at Oregon University. In addition, Franklin has been named the new CEO of the newly rebranded Mitchell & Leonard Partners firm. The firm made it through unscathed from the SEC.

Although Dani was unable to play in the State Volleyball Tournament, she did help Monica and Emma lead St. Lucas High to another State championship in Track and Field.

Lastly, Vivienne and Denise, the two matriarchs of the family started a foundation to promote equity, quality, and accessibility in advancing the policies of systems created to serve underprivileged children in the inner cities of Georgia.

C. F. FRANK

SONGS FOR REYNA

Connect and stay updated with C. F. Frank via:

ABOUT THE AUTHOR

C. F. FRANK IS AN AMERICAN AUTHOR OF NOVELS, ESSAYS, AND POETRY FOR AN ARRAY OF AUDIENCES. HE FIRST REALIZED HIS INTERESTS AND PASSION FOR WRITING IN HIS FORMATIVE YEARS.

A TENNESSEE NATIVE, HE IS AN ENTHUSIAST OF FILMS FROM THE GOLDEN AGE OF HOLLYWOOD, PRODUCING, AND NATURE. FRANK CURRENTLY SPENDS HIS TIME READING A BOOK A WEEK AND TRAVELING, BUT NEVER TOO FAR FROM A KEYBOARD, PEN, OR PENCIL.

www.ingramcontent.com/pod-product-compliance
Ingram Content Group UK Ltd.
Pitfield, Milton Keynes, MK11 3LW, UK
UKHW041845200726
13854UKWH00005BA/2148

9 781726 496353